1-13-2011

T
S

THE CHAINS OF SARAI STONE

Cynthia Haseloff was born in Vernon, Texas. She was named after Cynthia Ann Parker, perhaps the best-known of 19th-century white female Indian captives. The history and legends of the West were part of her upbringing in Arkansas where her family settled shortly after she was born. She wrote her first novel, *Ride South!*, with the encouragement of her mother. Published in 1980, the back cover of the novel proclaimed Haseloff as "one of today's most striking new Western writers." It is an unusual book, with a mother as the protagonist searching for her children out of love and a sense of responsibility, rather than from a desire for revenge or fame Haseloff went on to write four more novels in the early 1980s. Two of these focused on unusual female protagonists. *Marauder*, of the two, is Haseloff's most historical novel and it is also quite possibly her finest book. As one review put it, "*Marauder* has humor and hope and history." It was written to inspire pride in Arkansans, including the students she had known when she taught high school while trying to get her first book published. Haseloff's characters embody the fundamental values—honor, duty, courage, and family—that prevailed on the American frontier and were instilled in the young Haseloff by her own "heroes," her mother and her grandmother. Haseloff's stories, in a sense, dramatize how these values endure when challenged by the adversities and cruelties of frontier existence. Her talent, as that of Dorothy M. Johnson, rests in her ability to tell a story with an economy of words and in the seemingly effortless way she uses language. Haseloff once said: "I love the West, perhaps not all of its reality, for much of it was cruel and hard, but certainly its dream and hope, and the damned courage of people trying to live within its demands."

THE CHAINS OF SARAI STONE

Cynthia Haseloff

GUNSMOKE

This hardback edition 2010
by BBC Audiobooks Ltd
by arrangement with
Golden West Literary Agency

ISBN 978 1 408 46307 9

British Library Cataloguing in Publication Data available.

Printed and bound in Great Britain by
CPI Antony Rowe, Chippenham and Eastbourne

THE CHAINS OF SARAI STONE

Chapter One

The sounds of the guns were distant now, left back in the Comanche camp. Only the thudding strike of the horses' hoofs against the prairie grass and soil and their labored breathing filled the stillness. Behind him Hugh Kane heard the faint rattle of canteens and cups as a splinter of the dragoon detachment followed him away from the camp in pursuit of the escaping rider.

Kane dug in a spur. The big bay stretched out further, gaining on the iron gray Indian pony and its rider. The little rider flattened against the gray and picked up a pace or two. Kane's heart pounded in him. A strange fear — fear for the small rider's life — drove him. Kane was sick of killing. Behind him the dragoons thundered closer. He now raced Death across the empty land.

The great bay horse's strides ate the ground between him and the gray. Kane closed on the rider, reached out and caught the buffalo robe. It came off in his hand. He dropped it. The rider swerved away from the bay. It took Kane a moment to turn, and the Indian was ahead of him again.

A shot rang out from the dragoons. The gray turned again, back in her original direction. Kane spurred the bay. Again he came alongside the gray. He caught the rider about the waist and lifted, letting the gray run away. Kane blinked as the tip of a quirt glanced off his cheek. The rider squirmed and kicked. Fighting to pull the horse up, Kane lost his hold, dropping the rider to the ground.

As Kane turned, he saw that the little rider was a woman. She fell to her knees, thrusting out one hand to stop her fall, holding something against her with the other.

Another shot popped the air, and suddenly Kane was mad. He pulled his own heavy Colt pistol and fired in front of the dragoons' horses.

"You bloody, ignorant bastards, can't you see this is a woman?" he shouted. The dragoons pulled up. "Go on back. I'll handle this." The soldiers hesitated. Kane cocked the pistol again in the air so they could see. Finally, they turned away.

When Kane looked back, the woman was on her feet and running toward her horse. He cut her off, caught the blanket she had wrapped over her head and body. She released it, but it clung to her. Kane jerked her down. She fell awkwardly, twisting onto her side, keeping a child away from the weight of her fall. Holding the child tightly to her, she spun away.

"No shoot! No shoot!" she shouted keeping her body between him and the child. Her clothes were torn. The skirt split to her thigh revealed the long sinuous leg and the softly wrinkled moccasin.

Kane reined up and dismounted quickly. He caught the woman and turned her to him. Her blue eyes flashed a cold fire at him as a knife struck out at the hand that held her. Kane dropped his hold and stepped away to a safe distance.

"Why, you're a white woman," he said, almost to himself. Amazement washed over Kane, glazing the confusion of the fight and flight. "You're white."

The woman wasn't very big, but she was lean and fast. Her fair hair whipped into her eyes as she looked for her horse, the escape. Kane was between the rider and her horse. Her blue eyes watched him closely, looked beyond him at the waiting gray. The woman did not seem to understand his words.

"I won't hurt you," Kane continued softly, this time in Comanche. He pointed at his holstered gun and raised both hands slightly. "No shoot," he signed. He shook his head vigorously. "No hurt you."

Watching her steadily, he picked up the trader's blanket bordered with an intricately beaded band. He dusted some of the grass from it and held it out toward her. She stared at him; did not lower the double-edged knife.

"Baby get cold," he said, making a cradling gesture. The woman just watched him, deciding something. He offered the blanket again. Holding the child tightly to her with the hand that held the knife, she reached slowly for the garment. Her eyes never left Kane's face. When she had the blanket, he stepped away.

Hugh Kane was a man used to wild things. To get their trust, he knew to give them room and time. He stood there on the empty plain with the woman for several minutes. He did not move. The little Indian child had stayed silent and sober throughout the events, but now it began to shiver and whimper. The woman, feeling the shaking, looked down. Slowly she put the knife into the top of her moccasin leg and drew the blanket around the child.

Kane sighed. "That's a whole lot better, ma'am. We ought to get on back now." He remounted his horse and rode out to catch up the woman's horse and buffalo robe. Then they rode back to the burning camp.

The Ranger camp was quiet after the day's fight. Fires still smoldered among the Comanche teepees. Most of

9

the men were asleep, satisfied with the destruction of the village, the recovery of the stolen horses, and their plunder. Captain Jo Martin breathed slowly, hands laced across his chest, dreaming of the trophy he had won — the long-sought trophy — the lost white child now a woman, Sarai Stone. Martin slept comfortably, secure in knowing that the woman was safe in the hands of the men Silas Stone had sent to find her twenty-five years before.

"I give up hope," Jacob Logan said. "Back in '51 when I seen them two little boys and the way she looked at that damned Indian. She ain't got an ass-kickin' chance of making it ag'in with white folks. I said that then. It's all stout ag'in her."

"What about the promise we made to bring her back?" asked Hugh Kane.

"A promise are a promise. But I kinda figured that one expired . . . both ran out its time and died," Logan said.

"What the hell are we going to do then?" Kane pondered the thought he'd spoken.

Logan looked at the woman — blonde hair cut off Comanche style beneath her ears; blue eyes fixed on some distant spot that not only took no notice of them, but completely denied their existence. "Injun can do that," he said, turning the tip of a stick in the fire. "Make you disappear because he don't want you. They'd be plum easy killed like that. You ain't there, so he don't see you comin'."

"No," Kane said softly. "We can't kill her." And Kane thought, but did not say — no killing . . . not this time, Logan.

"No," Logan said, "I expect we can't do that. It's too late for it. But it would make things considerably simpler for everybody." He stirred the fire idly. "Silas never did say, 'It's over, boys, go on home and forget that promise you made me.'" Logan sat thinking. At last, he said, "Over yonder behind that gentle roll in the earth, there's a mess of Quohadi Comanches countin' out what happened here today, takin' care of the wounded, figurin' what to do, waitin' for us, and our guns, to leave so they can come back in here and see the truth and bury their dead. She knows it. She knows when we go to sleep, she can go back real easy.

"If she's here come morning, she's going back with us. Cap'n Martin will see to it. We'll have to take her to Silas. Be a shock to the old man. I expect even Silas gave up hope after we told him the situation with the children and the Indian." Logan rolled up in his blanket, hunched his shoulders and neck down away from the cold night's breath. " 'Night."

Kane looked at Logan's back, wide at the shoulders, thin and hard as iron. "It's best if you get some sleep, too, Kane," Logan muttered. "This ain't just our business any more."

Hugh Kane sat thinking of the course of the years that brought him and Jacob Logan to this day, this night, this dying fire. It began in San Jacinto the morning of April 21, 1836 — twenty-five years before.

It had rained all night as it had most of the time during the retreat away from Santa Anna, back toward the Sabine, the States. Houston made the Texians retreat, and train and retreat against Santa Anna's advance till the stringy men were nearly crazy from watching the women and children in carts and wagons, on foot, running away because nothing stood between them and Santa Anna's mercy. *Digüello*, the Mexicans called it. Uncon-

11

ditional surrender. Murder was the Anglo word, after Goliad and the Alamo.

Then, just as Houston expected, Santa Anna made a mistake — divided his forces because of the rain-swollen Brazos. Houston sent out runners, men like Kane and Logan, to call back the bitter deserters and the sick-hearted to fight, back to San Jacinto and the sluggish bayou. Logan and Kane had made the call and turned back, heading for the fight. When Kane's horse pulled up lame and Logan's was too tired to carry both men, they stopped for the night with a party of ragged women and children.

Kane was a boy, then, just fourteen, orphaned by Santa Anna's men at the Alamo and bequeathed to Logan by Doc Kane before he went to meet the Lady Liberty and found the death he expected. In that time, men said and believed that the flower of freedom was watered by a patriot's blood. And the price did not seem too high.

The rider from Stone's Crossing came in just as Kane and Logan finished breakfast with the fleeing women. "Give me a horse," he said. "I must get to Silas Stone. There's terrible news. Indians hit us. Massacre. God A'mighty." He was seeing it again as he spoke. "Stone's wife's killed and two of his sons. Indians took his grand-children."

Logan and Kane did not yield their horses, but carried the news to Silas Stone themselves after the fight. And that's how it began. Stone stayed to protect the now captured Santa Anna because he had promised Houston and because the infant Republic's credibility as a nation and not merely a rag-tag filibusterers' mob rested on the Mexican's life. Logan and Kane became Silas Stone's agents, trading among the Comanches, ever seeking the lost children. Women were taken, too, Lucinda Garrett and Rachel Stone, poor dear dead Rachel. Kane's eyes misted again for lost Rachel, dead now more than twenty years.

Within the first two years they got the women back. Rachel died. Logan grieved. Kane went back to the States, New Orleans, to study medicine in the new school there. Logan hunted alone then, blown about by the words of traders or travelers or friendly Indians. Kane came back as a doctor when the war with Mexico started. They both saw Buena Vista and Mexico City. When it was over, they headed for the Llano Estacado, the Staked Plains, for air to breathe and to search again. Years passed.

In '46, ten years after the search started, they found the boys — John and Jamie — and bought them outright from the Indians to the boys' chagrin and delivered them to Silas. One was twelve, the other fourteen. One stayed. One went back to the Indians before Silas got him home.

By then, hunting the lost had become Logan's and Kane's life. They didn't know how to stop. The lost child was a presence in their lives. On several occasions, they found other captives belonging to other families. They learned the ways of the Santa Fe traders, the Comancheros, the Comanches, and the vast land. Much of the time they worked as surveyors of the opening land or scouts for the Army, looking for a route for the California gold-seekers or just describing the unknown land taken from Mexico. And Kane practiced medicine wherever it was needed, keeping a small office at Belknap.

Finally, the girl turned up, a woman now. She simply came into an Army survey camp with a Comanche man and two little boys. He would not sell her, and she would not leave her family. That's when Logan gave up hope.

The lost child from Stone's Crossing: she was just right, where she was. Blinded by the long pursuit, the men had not expected that. Taking her back would have been a cruelty the two seekers could not sustain. She did not belong to white people any more, not even to Silas Stone. The thought of restoring her to her former life was over.

The Rangers had drawn them into this pursuit and fight three days before. Leaving their rods and chains and wagons, they rode with the Rangers, a detachment of dragoons, and other volunteers to this place on the Pease River looking for stolen horses — just horses.

Kane looked up. The scattered fires of the Ranger camp burned bright and hot on buffalo chips, holding off the cold night and empty prairie. A few men still talked around the fires. All in all, they had had a lot to be satisfied about. That day on the Pease they found the Quohadi Comanche winter camp and destroyed it, without casualties to themselves. They recovered seventy-three head of Texas horses and the lost child, Sarai Stone. Yet Kane was not satisfied.

"Get some sleep, Kane. Leave things sift out till morning," Logan said, and shifted in his blankets. "Dad burn, it's cold."

Across the fire, Sarai leaned back against the saddle and bags they had taken from her horse. Her youngest child slept against her beneath the ornamented buffalo robe. The voices of the coyotes and wolves searching the Comanche village among her dead hurt her. The scalps some of the men wore in their belts did not help much, either. Scalping, Sarai believed, caused the soul of the dead to wander between the winds, lost, incomplete forever.

She did not mourn or cry out, but silently rode the waves of sadness that swept over her again and again, pulling loose her hold on the shore of the living. If she chanted the death song, the white devils would know her family had been hit hard. This would give them comfort because her family was powerful. Nobah, her husband, was a leader of the Quohadi. He took the role after Soldier's Coat was killed at Antelope Hills. Sarai knew Elimah, her mother, was with the dead. She was not sure of the others, but many had died.

The thought of her sons, Topnah and Prelox, troubled her more than the dead ones she knew. She had not seen their bodies and that for her was hope. If they lived, they were somewhere in the black, cold night. The boys had gone out to hunt before daylight. She wondered if they were far away when the attack came. She wondered if they had seen their grandmother killed. She wondered if they were cold, hungry. She wondered if they had found safety among the other bands. She struggled to quiet the thoughts before they ripped a cry of pain from her, a cry the white men could hear and glory in.

If their father was dead — and she believed he was, or he would have come for her — if their father was dead, if their uncle was dead, the children were orphans. Without a family, without the band, they would have to make a new place for themselves, prove themselves quickly. The older boy, Topnah, was fourteen, old enough to know things, living skills, the band hierarchy. He was his father's and grandfather's child — born and raised to be a chief. The struggle would make him better. But the younger boy was still a child at ten.

15

Sarai had been alone at ten. She remembered the days of being between worlds — still white, becoming Indian. She had had Elimah, beloved mother.

Prelox, the younger boy, would suffer without the two women. They spoiled him, dressing him like his older brother in fine beaded buckskins and moccasins. Just as the dandified young men wrapped their oiled and braided hair in the fur of mink and otter and set their scalp locks apart in defiance of anyone who might try to take them, the women ornamented the child's hair. They braided tiny silver and brass bells into the small scalp lock that hung over his clear forehead. Comanche mothers, all Comanches, spoiled the boy children. It was believed that they might die soon as young warriors on raids or as young defenders of the village.

Sarai was a Comanche woman. Since she was ten she had been among them. She forgot most of her first life — the language, the dress, the conventions of behavior. The Comanche family replaced the mother and father she saw fall when the Kiowa and Comanche raiders swept into Stone's Crossing. The new family was complete with new parents, Soldier's Coat and Elimah. In time, their grown son became her husband. She bore him three children. Her life was complete with place and obligation in the community of the band and of The People, the Niminah. She released the white past, refused to return. Sarai was Niminah.

At first the Quohadi band kept her far away from the whites. But time passed. There were too many whites to avoid. And Sarai was Niminah. She concealed her whiteness whenever it was necessary at the trading places.

Sarai saw more and more of the whites and a contempt grew in her for their deceit and greed and exploitation of the land and other men. On the plains, she saw them violate the sacred earth, piercing it with iron plows. At the forts, she saw the traders cheating The People, selling bad food that made the children sick. White men tried to steal ponies for raw whiskey that took away The People's dignity and independence. The whites said that the Indians were bad for stealing and killing, but they took what they knew was stolen and sold ammunition and guns for the killing.

Elimah held Sarai close to her when white men, famous for their lust and abuse of Indian women, were near. She warned the child and watched over her. The Antelope Comanche women were not the wretched squaws squatting outside the forts. They held themselves high, kept away from the strange men, never raised their eyes or opened their mouths if white men came into the camp. They were women of The People. The race was in their bodies, and they held it dear.

Sarai never saw any good from the white race when she was with the Comanches. She erased the white from inside her. Sometimes the whiteness of her own body startled her.

Chapter Two

Sarai watched the men leave the fires and curl themselves in sleep, one by one. The one who watched her did not sleep. She knew this man and his companion — Healer and Quick-to-See, the Indians called them. She had known of them for many years. The word of their search passed among the bands. But she believed they had given up after Nobah refused to sell her, and she refused to return with them. It bothered her that they were here at this place. It was as if their persistence had given her to them at last.

As a child, Sarai believed her grandfather would come for her. She rode every morning and evening to a place beyond the camp where she could look toward the Texas horizon from which he would come. The Indians gave her a name for this, Seeker. In time, Seeker rode out morning and evening with a different purpose. She rode to be sure that no one was coming. She heard of Hugh Kane and Jacob Logan. She dreaded their coming. But she knew they would come.

Perhaps it was not yet over. An Indian woman knew that sooner or later her adversary would sleep, and her chance would come. And there were many miles between here and where they would try to take her. Perhaps Nobah yet lived and would come for her.

She let herself sleep lightly as she waited and the dream came — the dream of a clock ticking, of a warm place full of love and safety, of hunger for that place. It was not an Indian place, but white, a cabin or house.

It was a secure place.

The dream always ended in the same way. Sarai was transported without knowing to a Comanche camp. She staggered and stumbled through the smoldering teepee poles and burned hide covers. She was again Seeker, looking for something she did and did not want to find. At last, she saw a small hand, a child's hand, beneath the ashes that had been her home. She fell on her knees and ran her fingers through the warm ashes to touch the hand of her child.

She always awoke shivering from a cold too deep to be warmed even by a summer night. Freezing, she knew she was trapped, held by The People's way.

The Comanches were a warrior nation. A man gained place and honor only from his acts of bravery and cunning against an enemy. A Comanche man did not grow old and retire like a storekeeper. There was no place for an old warrior except among the women and children. That was a horrible thought to the young men.

When her husband and son went out into the danger and death their honor required, Sarai waited; but the dream had undermined her acceptance of the Comanche road. She knew its end. She became discontented, hungry for a new way. When she expected her men's return, she now thought of the time when one or both would not return. When they returned, discontent walked with her as she dreaded the time when they would go out again.

The dream made her long to have her husband and children about her high on the plains where game and grass and water were plentiful, far away from the white settlements, alone with the distant mountains and valleys, beside the cold, clear streams. The dream was to live in a different way, not the Comanche way she knew.

The dream solved nothing, but made her discontent with what she had accepted and loved most.

The dream was new. But surely it had grown in her over the years of battles and wounds, over the years of unrelenting inroads by the whites, over years of slow changes in Nobah who sometimes thought more of killing white men and dying than of living.

The dream came to her again and again after the fight at Antelope Hills when white men began to come deep into Comancheria. Soldier's Coat died there. Death entered into their household. She believed it would now find them all one by one until she found the child's hand in the ashes of the teepee. When she was awake again, the dream also made her remember things she had forgotten, wanted to forget — foolish things like a red hen in a straw nest or the smell of yeast bread or the little etched pictures in a book. For a long time she did not mention what she dreamed or what she saw. Finally, she spoke to Elimah of the dream and the discontent it brought. And her Indian mother listened silently, looking at the prairie beyond the rolled-up teepee bottom.

"It is another world that talks to you," Elimah said. "Your white blood calls out to you."

"I have taken another road," Sarai said. "Why does it talk to me now when I am happy with my husband and children?"

"So that you will know its voice when the time comes," answered Elimah. "It is often so. Perhaps the voice has much to say to you."

"I do not want to hear what it says. I want to be as I was . . . happy," Sarai said.

"You cannot be as you were. You are different. But I have raised you, and you have had a good heart to learn. I believe you are Niminah enough to accept your road and to remember The People," Elimah said.

Sarai awoke shivering with the dream. She lay still, listening to the camp sounds, recalling where she was. The fire was almost dead, just embers. All the men slept. The guard on the hill sat with his head slumped forward. Easy prey, Sarai thought. She drew her daughter to her and rose silently. She walked softly through the sleeping men. In a few moments she was beyond the last firelight in the sheltering willows.

Her moccasins left empty places on the thick frost. There was no time to hide the tracks, but along the river banks there would be less frost. It would seem as if she went to drink or bathe. She could lose the trackers there. Sarai moved swiftly down the red clay banks to the river's edge. The river bed was wide and flat with a run of water to the banks after the recent rains. In summer, Sarai could walk across this river, without wetting her feet, but not this night.

She hoped the Rangers would think she headed west toward the greater bands. They would search in that direction. She would go another way, cross the river going north. In time, she could move along the far bank following the twisting course back to her children.

During the afternoon fight, Sarai had been at the river. After she and Elimah packed the travois with the family's teepees and belongings, she was dirty. She went to the river to wash and to water the gray horse before they moved on. Sarai saw Comanche riders cross the river twice, in a panic, confused by the Rangers' sudden attack into their deep country. She heard the first shots and saw the young men ride into the water. She looked for Nobah, saw him leading the attackers away from the women — west to the hills where the men could gain time and fight. Her mind now saw the height of water on the horses' legs in the water.

Now she sat her daughter down under the tree, kneeled and pulled the heavy buffalo robe from her shoulders. She lifted the child into it and gathered it over her. Sarai stood up and pulled her long cloth skirt through her legs and under her belt into a kind of trousers. Finally, she looked across the river again for some tree or marker to place the shallow ford in her mind. Crossing thigh deep water would be slow. Tonight the water would be cold, nearly freezing. Finding the shortest, shallowest route occupied her whole body, every sense.

Suddenly, someone had her from behind, a great hand across her mouth. As he pulled her back, she felt her feet go out from under her on the bank, scattering rocks and dirt that fell into the water. The man dragged her from the tree even as her hands grabbed for it. He threw her against the sloping path as he shoved the sleeping baby toward the water with his boot. Sarai got to her hands and knees. Lifting herself, she lunged toward the water's edge. Her hands reached through the rocks and sand for the bundle that held the child.

But again the hand was on her, catching her by the forehead, bending her neck back. She shook free. The hand came down over her nose and mouth, smothering her. She gasped for air, grabbed the hand to pull it free. She saw the long blade of the Bowie as the attacker's free hand came up over her own.

Sarai pushed the blade away, still struggling in the man's death grip. She drove herself against him, her legs pushing against the tree. He fell back heavily with her weight, but held on, hitting her ribs with the butt end of the knife handle. She felt the pain shoot through her in a burst of light, burning up her whole side.

She was on her back, lying against the man's chest. The knife blade was against her throat. She felt it cutting into the left side of her neck, her throat, felt the blood flow out warm, as he tried to set the blade and draw it across. Both her hands came up to her chest under the arm. She rolled her weight against the arm. In the silence, she heard the man's labored breathing and the sound of a gun cock.

"Let her be or pay the price," Jacob Logan said, and pressed the heavy pistol against her assailant's temple. Sarai's hands shoved the arm and the knife away from her throat. She spun out of his hold to her knees and crawled to the bundle on the water's edge. Holding the still sleeping child to her, she sat in the darkness as Logan struck a sulphur match against his belt and held it near the would-be-killer's face. "Do I know you, fella?" he asked. "What business have you about this woman?"

Other men came to the top of the embankment. Captain Jo Martin and Hugh Kane held fire-brand torches and pistols. "What the hell's going on here?" Martin asked.

"This bird just tried to kill the woman," Logan said, pulling Sarai to her feet. He caught and gripped her arm tightly.

"Who are you, man?" Martin asked, sick inside with the sudden realization of what had nearly happened. The man remained silent. His eyes defied Martin as he spat tobacco juice onto the ground. "Speak up," Martin said. Kane waited beside him, intent on the scene.

"Name's Caleb Matthews," the man said finally. "And, by God, you'd best let me be." He picked up his hat, dusted it, and slapped it on. Caleb Matthews started up the dirt bank, shouldering past Logan who held his pistol down at his side. Ranger Captain Jo Martin stepped across Matthews's path, blocking his ascent. "Just a damn minute, Matthews. You've an explanation to make."

"I owe you nothing. None of you!" Matthews sprayed his words at the gathering men.

"Ain't you the Caleb Matthews from Mexia? Yeah, you are. Your wife was carried off by Injuns a few year back," Logan said.

"What of that?" said Matthews. "It's happened to other men."

"She tried to go back to them until she . . . ," Martin started, but suddenly remembered the grim story. "Until she finally killed herself."

"That's right. She turned Indian. Squaw. Nothing but a whore. She shamed me everyday she lived and even now. Every buck in the band that came to our place had her again and again in front of me before they took her off to the others. I saw how she was. What kind of man could put up with that? She wasn't fit to be among decent people, but I made the Christian mistake of trying to forgive her. I kept bringing her back. But that weren't what she wanted. She wanted them bucks."

Caleb Matthews whirled suddenly, pointed his finger at Sarai. "That un's just like her. Choosin' to live with a filthy red nigger, have his nits. She brought proof of her whoring ways with her in that papoose. It's better off her folks'd be if you let me kill her. Be a kindness to 'em."

Matthews's voice broke. Wiping at his face with a tattered coat sleeve, he dropped his gaze to the ground. "Let me pass, fellers."

"Go on. Get out of here," Captain Martin said. He knew a lot of the men felt sympathy for Matthews's unforgiving words. They believed it would have been a mercy if the long lost white daughter had died with the Indian women. But they would do nothing. It was not their way to mix in kin business.

"Is she hurt?" asked Kane.

Logan pulled Sarai into the light, turned her head to see the wound, wiped it with the last three fingers of his gun hand. "He cut a place on her throat. Looks some deep, but ain't long or into anything vital." He turned her about by the arm he still gripped. "She's scuffed up some."

"Logan, don't let her out of your sight," Martin said. "She's going back to Silas Stone alive. It's up to him whether he wants her or no." He pulled a folded white handkerchief from his coat pocket. "Here. Use this to bandage her throat."

Kane took the handkerchief. Martin went back toward the fires. "Come on, Logan," Kane said. "I want to look at the wound." Logan and the woman followed him back.

"Don't know how much of that talk you understood," Logan said as they climbed the embankment. "But I reckon there's a few words you'll get to know soon enough." Somebody will make damn sure of that, he said to himself.

At the fire, Logan signed for the woman to sit. Kane had a canteen. The doctor's bag was open. Sarai looked at the contents, the shining instruments, and leaned away.

"Easy," said Kane.

The child in her arms kicked out. Kane opened the buffalo robe. He smiled and Summer smiled back. He looked into Sarai's eyes.

25

"I want to look at your wound," he said.

Kane shifted the woman slightly so that the firelight shown on the bloody wound at her throat. Logan held the torch high. Wetting a rag, Kane gently wiped the blood away. His attention focused on the revealed wound.

"Ain't too bad?" asked Logan, leaning in closer to see.

"No," Kane said. "Not bad."

He folded a small pad from the bag, laid it over the wound, then wrapped it with Martin's white handkerchief.

"Her hands is hurt, too," said Logan.

"Uhm," Kane mumbled, shifting his focus. "Hold out your hands."

Sarai lifted her hands. She could not control the shaking. She closed them quickly and drew them back against her. Kane pulled them back to the light. He gripped them firmly and looked into her face.

"It's over now," he said. "Release your hands."

He opened the clinched fingers and washed the abraded palms. The smell of the woman was soft and warm like a summer prairie. Kane wrapped each hand in a strip of bandages and tied it.

"Get some rest if you can," he said, helping Sarai to her sleeping place.

"Logan," Kane said turning back. "We have to take her back to Silas."

"That's so," said Logan. "Tomorrow I'll go back out to the survey and pick up the logs. Might as well make the trip do for two things and get them records in when I come. I'll line out the boys, and they can keep working. I'll likely catch up to you before you get to Stone's Crossing." Logan was already bedding down again.

"What were you doing down by the river, Logan?" Kane asked.

"Gettin' a drink of water, I expect," said Logan. "What else?"

Chapter Three

The door to Lou Winn's house popped open before Captain Jo Martin and Hugh Kane.

"Hello, Lou," said Martin. "We brought you something."

Lou Winn worked, clearing the supper table across the room. She laid down her dishrag and straightened up as Kane drew the woman, Sarai, into the room.

"Knew your and W's door was always open, Lou, to the unfortunate and battle weary. What with Kane keepin' his little office here, Belknap was the natural place to come," Martin continued. Lou Winn still stood, but closed her mouth resolutely. Martin went on, as he generally did with women, without allowing her to say anything. "Had us a little scrap up north and got her and her baby back from the Comanch'. Some say she's Sarai Stone, from Stone's Crossing twenty-five years ago."

The thick heat of the room hit Sarai. She felt dizzy and light headed, but Kane had her arm and ushered her into the room, closer to the blazing fire. She drew back.

"Don't fret, darling," said Martin. "Lou won't hurt you." His spurs clanked as he crossed the floor toward an iron bedstead in the corner. He snapped the shackle cuff band tightly over the rail. "Lou, she's bad to take off when you're not looking and hell to catch. We'll just put her here for the night and get back in the morning. I turned her pony into your pen already. W can put some hay out. Bring her on over here, Kane, so I can get home. I haven't seen my family in almost a month."

Kane spoke to Sarai and turned her by the shoulders, but she could not move. She crumpled, almost lifeless. Kane grabbed for her and the child, catching her about the waist with one arm and the child with the other. Lou was quickly across the floor. She took the child. Kane lifted Sarai into his arms and carried her to the bed.

"Guess the heat and not eating has gotten to her," Kane said, as he laid the woman on the quilted cover. Martin closed the second cuff bracelet shut over Sarai's limp outstretched wrist. "Damn, Martin. She's not a threat to anyone."

"Have to be careful. If she got out of here, I might not be able to answer for her safety. People are funny. You know how Caleb Matthews was," Martin said, going toward the door. "I want to make sure she gets back to Silas Stone alive. See you in the morning." The door closed behind him.

"Her throat was cut," said Kane. Seeing Lou Winn's worried face, he quickly added. "Not bad. I tended it, not too good but under the conditions. . . ." His attention rested on Sarai. He turned her head gently from side to side.

"Mrs. Winn, I could use some hot water and lye soap," Kane said as he bent nearer Sarai. He began to unwrap from her throat and head the bright Mexican scarf she had traveled in. Without looking, he drew a chair beside the bed and sat down. He removed the blood soaked handkerchief, causing the wound to bleed again.

Lou Winn called out to W who was already coming into the room, stuffing his nightshirt into his pants.

"Take this child while I help Kane," she said, handing the rumpled man the child.

Lou hurriedly brought a pan, soap, and water from her large tea kettle. She had been through this many times before with Kane and long before without him. She set Kane's bag beside him and watched over his shoulder for a few minutes before returning to W and the fretting child.

Carefully, Kane washed, clipped, and sutured the deep cut. Sarai did not move during the procedure. Exhaustion held her somewhere that pain could not reach. At last, Kane sat back but did not get up. "How's the child?" he asked, still studying Sarai.

"Fat and happy as a little bug," said Lou. "Has a moss diaper."

Kane looked up. "Where's W?"

"Feedin' your horses," Lou said, bouncing the baby on her hip.

Kane was not listening, but staring again at the woman. "Lou, put her back in that laundry basket and help me here? I don't like this woman's color. There may be wounds from the fight. Something I missed." I *must* have missed something, Kane said to himself.

Lou wrapped the child in a small light blanket and laid her on a pillow in the oversize wicker basket. She came to Kane's side. Together they undressed the sleeping woman. She was dressed in layers — robe, blanket, clothes on clothes beneath. Systematically they stripped away the garments. Lou finally cut away the last of the shirt sleeve to get it free of the shackle. Neither of them paid attention to the growing nakedness of the woman until there was nothing left to remove. Lou pulled out a thin covering sheet from the bedside table, but stopped and stood holding it.

30

"Why, Kane," she said, "this woman's beautiful."

"Um-hum," Kane said, but quickly forgot the lean womanly body for the black bruise on her ribs. "Cracked ribs, broken maybe." He ran his fingers gently over the battered ribs. "That must have hurt all day, every step the horse took. She never showed it that I saw." Kane glanced over the extremities. "Here's a place across her leg."

Lou covered Sarai, exposing only the leg where Kane worked. "Looks like a bullet grazed her. Let's turn her over and check the back."

Gently, he and Lou moved Sarai onto her side, rolling her toward the shackled wrist. "Damn Martin for his chain," Kane said. "Sorry. . . ." He did not finish the statement. "Look at her left shoulder." Lou leaned closer. A broad white scar ran down the length of the shoulder blade.

"How in the hell did she live through that out there?" Kane's fingers moved along the raised scar tissue. "Where do you suppose she got that? Not too long ago, I bet. A year, or maybe two," he said almost to himself. "Somebody did some pretty good doctoring, cauterized the length of it. Son-of-a-gun. Those Comanches can do some work sometimes."

As she slept, Sarai dreamed and, as she dreamed, she remembered.

She saw again how she had studied the farm yard. A man and woman were driving away. She watched them grow smaller and smaller and finally disappear in an undulation of the land. Her attention returned to the yard. A cabin, chicken pen, shed, and barn with a post corral sat at the edge of the wintry fields. Plowing had not yet begun on the raw land. It was still only an anticipation in the homesteader's mind.

Nothing moved in the yard or buildings except the penned-up chickens. Sarai had not eaten in three days, neither she nor Elimah nor her children, the boy, Prelox, the infant daughter, Summer. Their camp at Antelope Hills had been hit by Rangers, scattering the family. Soldier's Coat, her father, was dead. Her husband and eldest son were gone. Three days of walking brought the two women and children to this homestead. They traveled now toward the meeting place at Medicine Mounds, south and east of their winter camp.

Sarai watched the scene closely from her hiding place in a brushy draw cut by years of rain and wind. Elimah stood beside her. Her black eyes scanned the yard.

The hens in the tight little pen walked up and down the edges of their kingdom. With studied dignity, a hen turned one bright eye to contemplate a bit of corn or gravel at her feet. She scratched. Another hen darted across the pen after the morsel. Immediately the other birds took up the pursuit, thrashing about after the quarry.

"I will get a chicken," Sarai said, shucking the cradle board and baby from her shoulders.

"Wait a few moments more," Elimah said, continuing to watch the farm. "Farms have dogs. There may be a dog."

Sarai sat on the ground, holding the cradle board. Her fingers untied the bindings, and she lifted her daughter free. Brushing the plump cheek with her lips, she laid the closely wrapped bundle beside her eight-year-old son. "You stay here with your grandmother and Summer," she said. "I will go and see this farm. It may be there is much food about. We will have chicken to eat in a little while." Sarai put her shoulders back into the cradle harness. "I will fill this with good things to eat." She touched the boy's leg softly and smiled.

"Wait a little longer," Elimah said, glancing at Sarai who again stood beside her. "I do not like this. Such places are very strange, very dangerous."

"Mother, do you see any danger?" asked Sarai.

"It is not what I see," answered Elimah. "It is what I feel. I feel that this is a bad place for us. We should pass it by. Things have not gone well for us lately. I feel this place holds more evil."

"If we go on, the children will suffer. Already Prelox grows weaker, and my milk is not enough for the baby," Sarai said.

"It is an evil place," said Elimah, looking at her grandchildren lying together in the wash. "Go, then, but know the danger."

"Thank you, Mother," Sarai said. She quickly eased her body over the lip of the wash. She waited momentarily on her knees. Then she was gone across the bare expanse of ground to the side of the barn. She leaned against it, listening, and finally disappeared from Elimah's view. But Elimah still watched and waited.

Sarai was a woman of the horse. Like the other Comanches, she preferred to ride, shunned walking. She had been walking now three days. It was an unnatural thing for her, as shameful as the defeat at Antelope Hills. If she was hungry for food, she was also hungry to ride again, to possess again the power of swift movement, escape. She wanted a horse. The closed barn and empty paddock lured her as much as the strutting chickens. Comanche raiders taught her the lessons of their raids. Where there was a farm, there were horses. Where the corral was empty, the barn held the horses. Horses were wealth and freedom and escape to the Comanches.

Since she was ten, Sarai lived among the herds of the Comanches. She had great knowledge of horses. Her eye was true. Nothing about a horse missed her notice — not the straightness of its legs nor the depth of its chest. She knew by looking at the length and shape of the hip muscle which horses could sprint, which could run for great distances. The great eye, the carriage of the ear, told her the animal's attitude and intelligence or treachery. She raised the war ponies of her men and kept them in top form.

Running her hands along the leg of an animal, she could detect the heat difference between sound flesh and pain. She had poultices and herbs to treat wounds and soreness. She had wisdom to breed and save back and judge a horse. Elimah taught her. As the wife of Soldier's Coat, she managed his horses skillfully. Sarai took to it at once and did it well. In time, her running horses beat the soldiers in raiding pursuit and at the casually intense races at the rendezvous and forts. Sarai grew rich and generous gambling on the races with the other women. Horses were Sarai's strength and her weakness.

Now her weakness pulled her first into the barn, not to the pantry or chicken yard. Sarai slowly opened the door, just wide enough to slide her body inside. Quickly her eyes adjusted to the interior darkness. Daylight trickled in through the random boards. The barn was small, the front half work space and wagon shed; at the back were two stalls and a hall.

A soft whinny beckoned Sarai. She went swiftly toward it. In the half light she saw the riding horse. Quickly she ducked under the stall's single board gate. In a moment she had the horse's head and was stroking it. Another moment and she was running her hands over its body, down the back and legs. Sarai smiled to herself.

34

It could carry them all. At least, they would bring back a good horse from their defeat.

She left the horse and slipped out of the barn across the yard to a little shed hidden from earlier view. Sarai pushed the door open. The sweet smell of smoke filled her nostrils. From the ceiling hung cloth wrapped slabs of meat, shank hams, bacon. Sarai took a long ham shank, but held it away from her as she placed it in the cradle board. Pig meat offended the Comanches. Unless the house held nothing to eat, she would not eat the ham.

Lifting the latch silently and stealing inside, Sarai entered the cabin. She had not been inside a settler's home since she was a child. Her heart beat inexplicably faster within her, faster than all the stealth and danger her search brought. Yet there was nothing to fear in the quiet cabin with its softly ticking clock. Sarai spotted a cupboard. It surprised her a little that she knew so easily where to look for food, what to expect.

Again she slipped out of the cradle on her back. She spread a flour sack dish towel on the table and filled it with double handfuls of flour from the cupboard. She wrapped it carefully, tightly, tying the ends. She put it into the cradle board. She dusted off the flour on her hands with a towel lying on the table. Looking around, she saw a round loaf of bread and laid it beside the cradle board sack.

In the midst of the table a white cloth lay over something. Sarai lifted it. A roast of venison, cooked and partially eaten; a bowl of peas waited for some diner to come. Fork, knife, plate, and cup waited. Something in Sarai's mind told her the food and unused utensils anticipated an arrival.

A bird call, a signal from Elimah, fluttered across

the air. Sarai rolled the roast in the cloth and squeezed it into the cradle. She slipped it back onto her shoulders, picked up the loaf of bread, and opened the front door leading across the yard back toward Elimah and her children.

Sarai circled behind the smoke house, looking at the barn door which now stood ajar. Silently she slipped past, seeing the protecting wash only yards ahead. A great weight hit her, knocking her onto her face. Pain shot through her shoulder. Sarai lay still, stretched on her stomach.

Through the mist of pain, she saw her son dart out of the brush, running toward her. A black shape stepped between them, blocking her blurred vision of the child. A glint of sharp light darted into her eyes. Struggling to her elbows, she wiped her eyes. Between the two outspread legs, she saw her son running to her. Elimah ran behind him trying to catch him, stop him. Again the light darted at her. Sarai looked up at the glistening blade of the upraised axe, upraised against the child, waiting for him.

Sarai came staggeringly to her feet. Her trembling hands found the knife in her belt. The movement caused the axeman to turn. Even as he did, arms upraised to swing the bloody axe again, Sarai sprang against his chest, plunging the knife with both hands into his heart, pulling it deep with her falling weight.

Sarai lay spent on the ground, holding herself with her right arm. Above her the man's hands released the axe handle. The axe fell solidly, solemnly onto its iron head behind him. The handle swayed erect for a long moment, then fell to the side. The man's hands came to the knife protruding from his chest. He pulled it away, throwing it against the barn as he wove about in the sky above Sarai. His eyes were on her.

"White," he said. "White woman." Finally he fell straight and stiff before her.

Sarai felt the wet warmth of her blood on her back. She looked at her hands, holding her from the ground. On the inside of her left wrist little rivulets of her blood ran down into the red dirt. More blood ran over her hand, between the long, outstretched fingers. The world was strangely silent.

Sarai lost all sense of sound in the outer world. Only the sounds of her breath and beating heart came to her. She tried to stand, but surprised herself by falling instead of rising. Again she tried and this time rose to her knees, but her leg would not come forward, and up, to lift her.

Elimah had her, speaking softly. But Sarai could not hear or understand. The Comanche woman cut the straps from the cradle board, and its heavy weight fell away. The meat and backing board were cut through by the axe. Carefully, Elimah lifted Sarai's split shirt from the bloody wound. The axe's blade had cut a long gash into the flesh beside the shoulder blade. Without the board and its contents, the shoulder would have been split to the chest, away from the body.

Elimah lifted Sarai from her knees to her feet. She stood holding Sarai erect, looking about the farm yard. The door to the house was open. Firelight flickered against the interior darkness. Elimah had never been inside a house, but she wanted fire and some place out of the changeable weather for Sarai and the children. She decided. With the boy's help, she walked Sarai into the cabin, then sent him back for the baby.

Elimah lowered Sarai onto the hearth near the fire. She tore away the sleeve and shirt from the shoulder.

She found water and towels, wiped the wound, saw it, covered it, and leaned her weight against it. Sticking the poker into the depths of the fire with her free hand, she waited for it to become red hot. All the while she waited, she prayed and pressed the folded rag against the wound.

Sarai was conscious of the ministrations of Elimah. She rested her head on her right arm and looked into the fire.

"Does the bleeding stop?" Sarai asked.

"No," Elimah answered. "The wound is clean and only deep in one place thanks to the cradle, but it bleeds."

"You will have to burn it, like the old trapper did the Mexican at the Kiowa camp," Sarai said. The Comanches were close observers of techniques for treating wounds for they were often wounded and needed the information. In fact, they were well known on the plains for their ability to treat wounds and broken limbs.

"I will burn it," said Elimah. "When the iron is hot."

"The children are safe?"

Elimah looked at the small boy sitting on the corner bed, moccasined feet dangling high above the floor. He held the baby. "They are safe," she said.

"When you are done with me, hide the dead man in the wash. The other man and the woman will not be back perhaps tonight. I saw him put a traveling bag into the wagon, and there were winter pelts in the back. It may be they go to trade in a distant place. If they come back, take the children and run away fast. They will not hurt me. They will think I am white. That one called me 'white.' I will come to you again when I can."

Elimah listened to Sarai's soft voice. "I will take

the children," she said, turning the poker rod in the fire. Satisfied at last with the rod, she lifted it with the towels and rags and pressed it against Sarai's naked shoulder. Sarai jumped, but kept silent as Elimah's hand pushed her back against the floor. Then, Sarai was gone away in the pain and healing. Elimah fed the children and dragged away the dead man.

Later, during the long night when Elimah watched beside Sarai, Death seemed very near. She knew him so well — but familiarity had not made him her friend. He had taken too many for too many seasons for that ever to be. She saw their familiar faces in the firelight — her family, young men dead in battle, young women dead in childbirth, the Mexican girl who fell from the rocks, the feeble sick, the burned bodies in the Indian camps and homesteads.

Soldier's Coat came to her, young again, riding across the plains, his naked thighs gripping the spotted pony. Elimah's heart followed him, her horse beside his as in life. An endless land stretched before them, a bountiful land. He showed it to her.

Even as she washed Sarai's face, Elimah longed for that other land where so many waited. And she began to think how foolishly she had hated and feared Death when it came and took them away. Now she welcomed Death for he would bring her again into their midst. She would miss her son, Sarai, and the children, she thought. But one day when their journeys ended, they would come, too. She would wait for them there with the others. They would be together again with all The People. And they would bring others, unknown now to Elimah, but bound to her in blood and love. And the family would grow, unfurling through endless time in the endless land. There was no end.

39

"Mama," Sarai said in her sleep. Elimah had not heard the word since Sarai was new with The People, fretful in her child dreams. Elimah saw the bridge the girl made. Two peoples drew together across her. And the family was a double chain winding back and forth in time. All hate and fear were gone. Only blood and love joined them.

Sarai twisted under the blankets. "Mama. Papa," she said. "I'm home. I've come home." Elimah did not understand the meaning of the words, but she knew that this night Sarai, too, traveled in another land, another time.

Chapter Four

Kane sat at the kitchen table with W, drinking Lou Winn's coffee from a crockery cup. He let the steam and smell be drawn into his face. An empty plate that once held eggs and bacon sat before him.

"You look tired, son," said W Winn.

"Yes," Kane acknowledged. "I am tired."

"I'll make up the bed in the room for you," Lou said.

"That would be good," he said. "But I think I ought to stay in here. I'll sit in the rocker. Step outside and get some air now and then."

"I could watch for you," said Mrs. Winn. "You know I've watched many a night before you were a doctor. You won't be much good, if you keep going now. Besides, I can bathe her. Maybe get her to eat something."

"Like you did Rachel," Kane said.

"Like I did Rachel," said Lou quietly. "Don't think on Rachel. That was almost a hundred years ago. None of us has mentioned her name since. Why, I'd 'most forgot."

"You haven't forgot . . . neither of you. And neither have I. I was feedin' in Logan's lean-to barn," Kane said, remembering the fourteen-year-old boy he was. "I could hear you talkin' to Rachel. She hadn't moved off that corner rope bed or said a word to Logan or me in the four days since we got her to the cabin. Logan and I were at the end of what to do. Then you two showed up, creeping up the road, wagon loaded to the gunnels. You took hold, Lou. Most natural thing for you to get her to eat and talk."

Lou's eyes misted. "We thought she was going to be all right then if she just ate. We did not know then the darkness of her mind, the depth of her injury."

"You knew she was pregnant," Kane said. "I heard you tell her to eat for the child if not for herself. Red nigger child, she called it. Said she did not know whose child it was. And you, Lou, you said without a pause, why it's your child and it's God's child. You told her it was her chance . . . the chance to overcome evil with good."

"That's a long time ago. I disremember what I told Rachel," Lou said, embarrassed by Kane's memory. "Little pitchers have big ears, I guess."

"The ears could have heard different words, Lou," Kane said, and thought: *but not from you.* "I wish Rachel had listened. How she must have hated that child."

"No," Lou said abruptly. "Don't say that, Kane. No woman can hate the child she's carrying."

"Maybe," said Kane. "Maybe she loved the child in the end, took him to her, but she sure hated the Indian father."

Lou sat down with her hands under her apron skirt. "It was a brutal thing to bear . . . conceiving a child by the men who tormented her so long and cruelly."

Lou's fingers softly gripped the toes of the child kicking in the basket. She smiled. "Ain't you the pretty one," she said. "You got pretty blue eyes just like your mama."

"My God, this is strange," Kane said. "Rachel hatin' the Indians so, and this one fightin' to stay with them, keep the baby safe." He sighed.

"Ain't strange," said Lou. "Rachel was a grown woman

taken against her will, abused, sorely treated, shamed. Sarai was a child . . . favored and cared for. She grew to womanhood among the Comanches. They were her people, not her shame."

"It's different ends of the same log," W added. "One in the fire, the other not."

"Logan," said Lou, "this must go hard for Logan. Where is Logan, Kane?"

"He's coming. Went to get the survey logs to record," said Kane. "He'll catch up before we get to Stone's Crossing." Kane looked at his hands. "He wanted to kill the woman."

Lou and W sat silently for a time. "Twenty-five years since the Crossing Massacre," Lou said at last. "Silas Stone must be an old man now. The lost child is a grown-up woman with a child of her own. You and Logan have hunted a long time, and now you've found her at last."

"We didn't find her," Kane said quietly. "We converged. Logan and I quit looking sincerely about ten years ago when we were working for the Army. She and a Comanche man and two little boys just came into the camp. They weren't in any hurry, and they were curious. We tried to buy her. Nobah, that's the Indian, wouldn't sell. Then we tried to coax her to come back. We told her Silas wanted to see her, wanted to know that she was all right. She said tell him she was well and happy and that she could not leave her children and husband."

"Do you think she was afraid to come back because of the way people act toward a white woman who's been among the Indians?" asked W.

"I don't know that she would know that," Kane said. "She was just a child when she was taken. She hasn't

43

been around white people. Doesn't know their prejudices about that kind of thing. Indians for all their savagery are not shamed by miscegenation generally. Oh, there's some sexual shame among them for incest or for a woman passed over the prairie,' a woman used by all the men. But I don't think that's why she didn't come back. No, I think she loves the Indian and likes being a Comanche."

"Life is strange," Lou Winn said after a few moments. "You found her when you quit looking. She doesn't know she's an object of pity and scorn for living among the Comanches. Wants to stay with the Indians because she wants to, not because she's ashamed. Wonder how it will come out?"

"I wonder, too," Kane said. He drank the last of the coffee looking at the wall. "I wonder what Ben Stone will do?"

"Ben," said Lou. "The preacher . . . Rachel's husband? Dreadful man."

Kane rubbed the back of his neck. He said, "That's what he was twenty-five years ago. We'll soon know if he's changed." Kane stood up.

"There's a nightshirt on the bed," Lou said.

Kane nodded and walked toward the lean-to room.

Lou looked into the large clothes basket that held the sleeping child. The two-year-old was dark skinned but the hair was not the raven black of the Comanches and the eyes, when open, were a deep blue. The child was the proof for all the white gossip of Sarai's Comanche past.

"Well, my dear," she said, "all hell is about to break over your pretty head and your mama's."

Chapter Five

When Sarai awoke, Lou Winn stood above her. "Are you hungry?" asked Lou, rubbing her stomach and acting as if she put food into her mouth. "Hungry?"

Immediately Sarai sat up on her elbow to survey the room. She drew the sheet across her. "Baby," she said. "Give back baby."

"There!" Lou said, satisfied. "You do speak English. I knew you could not have forgotten."

As Lou spoke, Sarai swung her feet out of the bed and stood up, pulling the sheet with her. The chain caught her. She looked at it, jerked it. Feeling betrayed, Sarai became very angry. Her eyes flashed at Lou, and she flung the water pitcher across the room. A steady stream of Comanche words spilled from her.

"Kane. Kane!" Lou Winn called out, fleeing toward the door. "Kane!" She opened the door. "Kane!"

Hugh Kane ducked inside, dodging the missiles Sarai continued to hurl as she dragged the bed across the room.

"Easy now, lady," he said, moving slowly toward Sarai. "Go on, W. Get Martin and the key in here."

W. Winn hurried away after the Ranger captain. A glass crashed against the wall behind him.

Kane was cautious in his approach, but Sarai smacked him sharply on the side of the head with the metal wash basin. His hand went automatically to his face, and he backed away, looking for the blood he expected on his finger tips.

45

Suddenly Kane began laughing at himself and the scene before him — a naked, sheet covered woman, dragging a bed, hurling objects and curses about. "Logan would get a kick out of this. Whole place in full retreat before a woman wielding a wash pan. Good morning, Miss Sarai," he said. "Good to see you are feeling better. Nobody's going to hurt you, so settle down."

Sarai observed him closely. "Get baby," she said, advancing the length of the chain, dragging the bed closer. "Get baby!"

"Of course," said Lou. "We are idiots, Kane. The woman's worried about the little girl." Lou disappeared into the tiny sleeping quarters where she had put the child in the night. She gently picked up the little girl and brought her to Sarai. Just awake, reaching out for her mother, she was pleasant and smiling. Sarai took her but watched Kane closely. The basin was still in her left hand. Sarai sat down on the bed, holding Summer and the wash bowl.

"You're a sight," the doctor said and smiled.

The door opened. W. Winn reappeared. "Kane, Captain Martin is finishing breakfast. He'll be on over."

"No real hurry now, I guess," Kane said with a touch of cynicism. "She just wanted the child."

"That's what she said," Lou said. "I imagine Indians love their babies as much as anyone else."

"She's not an Indian," Kane said, looking at the white skin exposed above the sheet.

"Well, she's been raised and taught by Indians, That says something about them. At least, someone among them wanted her for their own child, raised her, taught her to love her child," Lou said. "A lot of the women in this very town draggin' babies around half naked and covered up with sores and lice don't handle their

46

children as well as that."

Sarai held Summer who stood on the bed against her.

Kane observed Sarai thoughtfully. "Comanches don't hurt their children," he said.

"Good Lord," Lou said. "She's practically naked. I'd best find her some real clothes before the men get here. Get her some bread and milk, W."

By the time Captain Jo Martin, his interpreter, Tom the Tonk, a traveling photographer, and a law clerk with paper and pencils arrived, Sarai was almost dressed properly. One arm and shoulder were bare, but Lou draped Sarai's Mexican scarf across the nakedness. Sarai sat comfortably on the floor beside the bed. Summer played peep eye beneath it.

"Sits on the floor half-naked like a heathen," Martin observed as he studied his prisoner, away from the wild country now and in the bright harsh light of civilization. "Makes me wonder whether I did the right thing bringing her in. Out there she seemed so fine and natural. Part of the land. Here," he shook his head, "here she just seems like a savage."

Kane raised up from the leaning position he had taken against the front wall as he watched Sarai. "She wouldn't be half-naked, if you hadn't chained her to the bed."

"I'll send someone back with the key," Martin said. "I forgot it rushing over here. Well, we might as well get on with the interview." Martin sat down in a rocker near the fire. "So the photographer can get his picture before he moves on. Are you ready to record our interview, son?"

The clerk nodded from his seat at the eating table. "You want to talk to her, Kane, or do you want Tom to?"

"As much as Comanches hate Tonkawas, she won't

say much to Tom. I'll talk to her," Kane said, coming forward to the chair by the bed and taking its back tentatively. Sarai looked up, but did not flare.

"Ask her name," said Martin, drawing the rocker into the circle.

Kane asked, and listened. "Her name is Blue Glass Dog, or The Woman Who Understands Death. The Comanches call her Seeker."

"Does she remember her white name?"

Kane made the query. "No. She only has an Indian name. Not white."

"Sarai Stone's her dad-blasted name," said Martin. "Try that on her." The question brought no response from Sarai. "All right, sister," Martin said. "Who do you think you're kidding? Let's try this, Kane. What is the name of her Comanche buck?"

"Nobah," came back through Kane. "Big man with the Comanches, Martin."

"I know that. Hot damn. We killed him out there on the Pease. She rode back and tried to save him, but we got him. Ask her if that isn't so," Martin pursued.

Sarai and Kane spoke a long time. Finally he said, "That's not the way she tells it. She says the man you killed was her husband's brother. But Martin, I told her Nobah didn't have a brother. So, then, she said it was her husband's uncle. She says she wanted to save her husband's uncle. Nobah got away clean."

"The man we killed was Nobah," Martin said. "You saw him."

"I saw the mess you made of whoever it was," Kane said. "Shotguns in the face don't leave much to recognize, Martin." Kane spoke to Sarai again. "She says it was White Wolf. You did not kill Nobah."

Martin's mouth twitched. "Tell her we've sent word

to her folks to come get her. And they will take her a long way away. She'll never see the prairie or a Comanche again. But we'll let her go back to the plains if she'll admit Nobah's dead for the record. We'll say she just slipped away."

"That's mean to offer," said Lou Winn under her breath. "Deceitful." Sarai's eyes darted over the woman's open face.

"Please, Mrs. Winn. This is important to the safety of the frontier," said Martin. "Well, Kane," he added impatiently.

"Well, what?" said Kane.

"Well, tell her we'll let her go if she admits he's dead."

"Do you mean it?" asked Kane.

"Hell, no."

"Then it's a lie, and I won't tell it," Kane said.

"Tom," Martin said. "Tell her. Kane, don't you open your mouth. She's on her own now. And don't make any signs, either."

Kane set his jaw and tipped back in the chair. Sarai looked at his face, stubbled with several days of beard, mouth drawn up to one side. Kane pulled at his lower lip with his right hand. Then he covered his mouth with it and watched Sarai.

The scout talked over Martin's deal with Sarai. "The baby goes, too?" he asked. Martin nodded.

The man talked intently with Sarai who sat studying Martin's clean-shaven face. Sarai did not talk to the interpreter. She just listened and watched Martin and the window beyond his shoulder. Noticing, Martin got up from the rocker and went to the window. He opened it a few inches. "Awfully warm in here," he said, and returned to the rocker.

Sarai rolled her head idly against the side of the bed as she watched and listened. She did not trust Martin. His deal came too easily. He tempted her with his action. He offered too much with his words. Healer and the woman had quit talking to her. She tried to think what to say. She wanted the door to the stuffy little room to open. She wanted to climb on the gray and be away from these people. It was simple enough to do — admit Nobah's death, give his enemies his death on the ephemeral chance of her own freedom. She did not take her eyes off Martin.

An idea came into Sarai's mind. It was very important to this man to have killed Nobah — important enough to offer her freedom. The death of her husband was a prize to the white man. She would not give it.

At last she spoke through the interpreter. "She says she don't believe you'll let her just go after tying her to the horse and this bed. But she don't care. She's lookin' forward to meetin' up with her white folks. She decided comin' in she ain't going back to Nobah. He's gettin' old and mean and lately he's been beatin' on her and talkin' about gettin' a younger wife. She don't fancy being hit or havin' another woman come into her teepee. Letting his uncle get killed won't help neither. She's free of Nobah here. Back there she'd just get more whuppin'."

"He's dead," Captain Martin said to Sarai.

"That ain't they way she sees it, Capt'n," said Tom.

"Tell her to admit he's dead."

"She ain't goin' to talk any more about that, Capt'n," said the scout. "Look at it this way. If he's dead, she ain't got nothing to lose by 'fessin' up. You give her a chance to be free. On the other hand, if he's alive, she might say he ain't, so you'll let her get back to him, then you'd be tricked and never know. She'd most. likely enjoy that. On the third hand, if he's alive and he beats on her, she ain't got nothin' to gain by goin' back." The scout grabbed Sarai's arm and pushed up the sleeve. "She ain't mutilated herself like she would if she was mourning." He caught at Sarai's hair. She turned her head quickly to pull it out of his fingers. "Hair's cut some. Did you see her cut her hair, Capt'n?"

"It was like that when Hugh Kane brought her in," Martin said, crossing his arms across his chest.

"Well, they cut their hair off to show grief, but it must have been for somebody else, before. Did she wail or carry on while you was out there?" asked Tom.

"No."

"With my figurin' and the signs, Capt'n, I think you killed somebody else. You offered her too much to turn down without a damn good reason, like a mad Indian waitin' to beat hell out of her," the interpreter concluded.

Martin drew in a deep breath and released it in a sigh. "Nobah is dead. I know it. I know it, and that woman knows it. She's robbed me slick as a tin whistle after I saved her. That's gratitude! Go on, boy," he told the clerk. "You won't be needed further here."

"Maybe she don't know she's been saved," said Tom. "Likely she feels pretty cut off, chained up like she is."

Martin put his hands on his knees and forced himself up from the rocker, resigned to his stalemate with Sarai. "I can't see what she expects to gain by denying we killed Nobah. But she's had her say for now." Martin walked away slowly with his hands in his pants' pockets. He turned back at the door. He was smiling. "Maybe you outsmarted yourself, Miss Sarai," he said. "Tell her this, Tom. I'll have men watching. And if she takes off for Comanche country, I'll know for sure that Nobah's dead as a mackerel. I'll know. And I won't think nothin' of leading the Rangers against the Quohadi band without its leader. I know their tricks. I'll wipe them out. No survivors." He stood at the door with his hand on the knob.

Tom repeated Martin's words to Sarai. Her eyes never left Martin's face, never flickered or blinked.

"Kane, you can take her on to Silas tomorrow. I'm done with her unless something comes up by then. I'll send the key before you have to leave."

"I want the key now," said Kane.

"If that's what you want knowing her for a savage, I'll send it over. Folks know you are here. Some of them need doctoring," Martin said, opening the door. "Picture man, get your picture and move on."

The picture showed Sarai holding Summer on her lap and sitting unnaturally on a chair with a bare shoulder peaking out of the shawl whose fringed tail covered the manacled wrist. Part of the chain was exposed at the side of the little brown picture. The key arrived after the photographer folded his equipment and moved on in his dusty pursuit of history.

An unusual number of the citizens of Belknap had vague physical complaints that day. They came and stared at Sarai whenever Kane turned his back. Sarai sat at first on the floor, watching the visitors and the doctor.

"Why ain't that jest like a heathern. And a baby, too! Imagine bringing back the child. That's gall. No tellin' who the father is the way Injuns swap their women around. I heard she had three kids. Each one by a different buck, I bet," one thin town woman observed as Kane tried to count her fluttering pulse. "Imagine!"

He dosed her heavily with a purgative to remove the excessive bile.

After the woman left, Lou Winn closed the door and leaned heavily against it. "Imagine, indeed. There's too much imagining going on right now."

Lou crossed the floor to Sarai and began to pull her up. "Kane, tell her among white people it's a dishonor for a chief's wife to sit on the floor," Lou said. "Tell her she should sit on a chair to keep her dignity. Is there a Comanche word for dignity?"

"Well, there's *puha*, which means a kind of personal power," Kane said.

"Good. You say for her to keep it and sit here in my old rocker."

Kane explained Lou Winn's wish, and Sarai looked straight into the woman's eyes as he spoke. She considered the shapely rocker. The smooth wood and curved lines reminded her of a fine horse moving easily on the plains. Sarai handed the child to Lou, backed up to the chair and lowered herself slowly into the seat. The chair shifted back with her weight. Sarai leaped forward to avoid the fall.

Lou laughed brightly and put her free hand on Sarai's forearm. "My but you have so much to learn, dear. Look at me." Lou gestured to herself. She sat and rocked slowly. "It only goes back this far, unless you push too hard of course, but that's hard to do. It's rather like a rocking horse for grown up people. Tell her, Kane."

"I think she's got it," Kane said.

Sarai looked at the chair closely, tested it with her hand on the arm, attempted to tip it over on the long rockers, and finally sat tentatively.

"Rock now, Seeker." Kane nodded.

Sarai rocked.

"Very good," smiled Lou. "Very good, indeed."

Sarai began to enjoy the chair. She seated herself deeper into it and stroked the floor more widely and evenly. She smiled. "Good. Very good indeed," she said.

Lou held Summer out to Sarai, plopped her softly into her lap. "Babies love rocking chairs," she said. Lou glowed with success as Sarai and Summer rocked away the afternoon.

"It's just a rocking chair," Kane said.

"Oh, no, Kane. It's far more," Lou answered. "It's a beginning."

Chapter Six

In the heat of the winter day, Sarai removed the buffalo robe and threw it across the horse's withers beneath her child. The Mexican scarf, bright and cheerful, covered her cropped blonde hair. The long ends of the striped cloth trailed down her back over the blanket wrapped around her middle and over one shoulder. Her long skirt moved up leaving a few inches of white skin between the hem and moccasin top. She rode erect, perfectly at ease on the horse even with the child. She looked straight ahead. Her blue eyes never took note of Kane.

"By God, she looks like a Comanche," Kane said to himself. "Acts like a Comanche. She sure is not a ten-year-old white child."

They made an agreement, Kane and the woman, day before yesterday morning at Belknap. He would not chain her feet again beneath the horse's belly, and she would not run off. She would go to meet her grandfather, settle with him. Still, Kane kept the line on her horse.

Kane watched the flat horizon. The steady gate of the horse, the surprising heat of the day, the endless miles caused his mind to drift. He fought back. A man could not lose his alertness out here. Not now. Not with the woman. Kane knew she was a beloved woman. The hardy chance existed that somebody would come to take her back to the Comanche people. Where the hell was Logan? Someone to talk to would keep him awake, Kane thought. He got off his horse, deciding to walk for a little.

"You want to walk some?" he asked in Comanche. They communicated with a mixture of Comanche, Spanish, and sign language. Sarai ignored him. "That's right," he continued in English. "You Comanches don't walk . . . or talk. You'll excuse me, Miss Sarai, if I do. Keeps me awake in case somebody decides to take you back." Kane kept walking, talking, watching the empty land with narrowed eyes.

"Do you remember Rachel Stone? She was taken off with you children. Your aunt. Jacob Logan and I brought her back that fall after the massacre. She was a mess. Bull Back got her in the split after the raid. Her boy, Jamie, was given to another Kiowa. And when she had her baby, Bull Back himself dashed out its brains. The baby interfered with her ability to work for Missus Bull Back.

"Missus Bull Back was . . . how can I put this delicately? . . . not refined. She wasted no time on social communication. When she wanted something, she pointed or gestured and beat Rachel till she did it. Her fine young daughter, Miss Bull Back, took up where her mother left off. They burned Rachel. They beat Rachel. They used her as a beast of burden. And of course, at night, when Rachel was not tending the horses, Bull Back and his friends put Rachel to other uses.

"Logan and I found Rachel in Bull Back's summer camp in the White Mountains to the far west. We traded for her. We confirmed that you were with Soldier's Coat. And then, we came home because we had Rachel to care for. The year was turning, too. Snow would come in a month or two.

"We arrived at Stone's Crossing in the fall. The stockade was still up then. The little cabins of the settlers were built into the timber walls of the fort . . . three more walls, a roof, and a mud cat chimney on each one. The horse corral was rebuilt. And the bodies of your grandmother and your father and all the others had been laid to rest a long time in the new cemetery. Grass almost covered the raw dirt mounds. The cemetery was right by the gate so everybody saw it when they came in, so they knew the crime against Stone's Crossing. But that was little or nothing to the crime to come against Rachel.

"In the months of searching and in the months of returning, Logan and I had come to admire Rachel. As Logan said in his astute way, she was 'admirable for courage.' We nursed her through a spell of fever on the Colorado. We heard her stories of the captivity. And we, as strong men, knew we could not have stood what that woman endured.

"And yet there was a bravery about Rachel that was not just standing up to adversity, but an overcoming of it. She could tell in vivid detail of the flowers she had seen in Sonora, of the bushes on which every thorn was a fish hook. She carried the fish hook thorns with her as proof. Once she had been lost in a crystal cave somewhere in the White Mountains two days and a night. She described that cave with a detail and understanding that was both poetic and scientific. An angel, she said, ministered to her wounds there, and they never hurt again."

Kane walked, kicking the ground, thinking of dead Rachel. "Logan loved Rachel. He would never have said it then because she was another man's wife. But he did love her and later on he knew it. I loved her, too, as a boy loves who has never had a mother or sister.

"You don't understand diddle, do you?" Kane asked, studying Sarai's face as he walked. "That's good because I would never say such things if you could. Hell, I've never said them to myself."

Kane walked on, silent now, seeing the scene twenty-three years before when he and Logan returned another woman to Stone's Crossing.

Ben Stone was a newly married man. Word of his son's death from a trader brought a surety of his wife Rachel's demise. He assuaged his grief in the soft, full bosom of Jane Garrett, another survivor of the massacre who had been left behind when her sister, Lucinda Garrett Bond, a returned captive, and brother-in-law suddenly pulled out for the States.

Ben stood framed in the cabin door with Jane behind him. The three riders waited in the yard.

"I've brought your wife, Rachel, home," Logan said.

"My wife Rachel is dead," said Stone.

Kane looked at Rachel, but she still had the vacant gaze he had grown used to across the plains and miles. She was better now since the sickness on the Colorado, since Logan's tender care.

"She stands before you," Logan said, shocked.

"No," Ben Stone said. "My son and my wife were killed by Kiowas. We had the news in the summer. I remarried in the fall. Jane," he called gently. The young woman came to his side. "These are the men my Pa sent to help us. You men know he's still with the government?"

Logan sat up straight. Kane thought he might shoot off the horse the way energy jerked through him. His tired face bore the innocent imprint of pure puzzlement and astonishment. His mouth opened, then, closed again.

58

He plainly wanted to say something, but found nothing in his mouth to say. He tried again with the same results. "Well, damn," he finally managed. "Just damn. Ain't this a fix?"

"Thank you for your efforts," Ben Stone said, turning and gently shepherding his new wife back inside. "It's time for our lunch."

"Wait a minute," Logan said as he witnessed the departure. "Ain't you got nothing to say to this woman?"

Ben Stone looked critically at Rachel, his lost wife, brought back unacknowledged from the Kiowas. "I'm sorry for your condition, ma'am. God be a comfort to you." He looked back at the woman whose arm he held and smiled softly. His other hand reached for the heavy cabin door.

Logan leaped from his horse. He hit the door as it closed. "This ain't goin' to work, Stone. I've brought your wife Rachel back. Open this door." An interior bar dropped heavily across the timbered door. "Son-of-a-bitch," Logan swore.

The frontiersman turned toward the people of Stone's Crossing, but they were not there. Every door in every perimeter cabin was closed and barred against Logan, Kane, and Rachel Stone. A single hen worked the oat spillings beneath the horse trough.

"Indians are kind people compared to this nest of hypocrites," Logan said. "I ain't goin' to take this, Stone. Not by a long damn shot. You come back out here. I ain't brought you no stranger."

There was no response from inside the forted-up cabin.

"By God, I'll set fire to you and burn you out," Logan cried, searching his mind for a deed dastardly enough for the outrage.

He walked out into the empty center of the fort. He

turned slowly, looking at all the closed doors and shuttered windows. "If you'd been shut up this tight against the Indians, they'd have gone home empty," he mumbled. "By God in heaven," Logan shouted, raising his hand in oath. "This woman is Rachel Stone. Rachel Stone is alive. Rachel Stone bears witness against you . . . all of you . . . shits."

Suddenly Logan sat down in the middle of the empty yard. He jerked off one moccasin, then the other, and began beating them together, knocking the thick dust off. Kane almost laughed at the frenetic gestures and movements of his friend. Logan was like an angry squirrel, insulted on home ground, irate, re-marking its territory, re-ordering its world.

"There go, Christians," he yelled. "Lookey here. Everyone of you sneaks. See what I am doin'?" Logan slapped the moccasins together, threw them down, and began brushing the bottoms of his bare feet. "I'm knockin' the dust off my feet as testimony again' you. Take that, you Christian bastards. There ain't nothin' for you now but trouble. And you got it comin'."

When he finished the peculiar rite, Logan sat quietly thinking in the fort yard. At last, he re-gathered the worn moccasins and replaced them on his feet. He stood up and walked back to the horses. He shoved his foot in the stirrup and swung into the saddle. He stooped forward deeply at the waist and caught the lead rope on Rachel Stone's horse. Leading the woman, followed by the boy, Kane, he rode out of Stone's Crossing into the gentle embrace of the empty land.

"I sure never expected that," Logan said.

"What was that business . . . taking your moccasins off and all?" Kane asked much later.

"Oh, that," the man said shyly, wiping his stubbled

chin. *"That's from the Bible. Once in Tennessee I heard a hell-fire Methodist sermoning about Jesus telling the disciples to knock the dirt off their feet against any folks who would not receive them. He said it would go hard against 'em when Judgment rolls. I figured that bunch back there would get the meaning. Give 'em something to worry about. As it's so, they got it comin', too. Still and yet, they'll probably figure out I ain't exactly a full-fledged disciple. Still it ought to work against such folks. They kind of sour your stomach on religion altogether."*

Returning from his reverie, Kane said aloud to Sarai, "We took Rachel back to the Crossing. Your Uncle Ben had a new wife. So we went to Logan's place. That's where he killed Rachel."

Chapter Seven

As he walked, Kane's mind ran back through the years looking for the reason, the place where the killing began. That late fall, he and Logan brought Rachel home. They did not know what to do with the woman. Logan needed something to do, something for Rachel, so they began adding a separate room for Rachel, making a neat dog-trot cabin of Logan's old lone pen. But Rachel did not care. She lay on the bed facing the wall in the old cabin. She did not eat. Logan's despair grew as Rachel slipped away.

The Winn wagon lumbered serenely into the yard. Logan stood up and wiped his right hand against his leather britches. He walked to the wagon as it came to a stop. Offering his hand to W. Winn, Logan said, pumping the other's hand, "Why, W, you old scamp. Get down. Come on inside. There's food to be et for all."

W. Winn jumped from the wagon box and helped down his sturdy wife. Lou Winn was a wholesome woman. Her cheeks were full and pink beneath the summer's tan. She was small and solid, moving already toward a plump maturity. Her bonnet and dress went together and were well set and tidy even after the long trek. Mrs. Winn was a Texas woman full of love and hope on the one hand; practical and unfluttered by circumstances on the other. Not much done by mankind shocked her.

Logan almost hugged Lou. "You are the answer to a prayer," he said as the woman righted herself on the ground.

"How so, Jacob?" Lou asked, brushing her skirt into place. Kane had never heard anyone call Logan by his Christian name before.

"I've got a woman," Logan said.

"Oh," Lou said with interest.

"Not like that," Logan said quickly. "A sick woman. Silas Stone's daughter-in-law. And it's a helluva mess. Pardon my language," he said as an afterthought.

"Well," Mrs. Winn said, "it's plain to see you're full up and runnin' over with your thoughts, Jacob. Are you goin' to ask us inside?"

"I done that," said Logan. "I said there were eats for all."

Lou Winn looked closely at Logan. "Then, let's see to 'em and to your woman trouble."

She walked toward the cabin with Logan by her side.

Kane wanted to follow, to see what the little sharp woman would say, but he stayed and helped W. Winn unharness his team. "Go ahead, Mr. Winn," Kane said. "I've eaten, and I'll put 'em in the corral and feed them for you."

"Thank you, boy. It has been a long day. There's a sack of oats in the wagon . . . near the back," he said, stretching his tired spine. Winn went slowly toward the lighted cabin door.

Kane led the mules to the corral and turned them loose. They went straight to the water flowing through the corner of the corral. He got a bucket of oats from the wagon and spread it along the trough in the lean-to barn as the mules came up to feed. Sitting in the trough, watching the mules he could hear what went on in the house and see through the open half door behind him.

"How long since she's eaten?" Mrs. Winn asked.

"Shoot," said Logan, "she ain't et since we found her, not really."

Mrs. Winn looked at him, waiting for more particular information.

"She ain't et but a bite of cornbread in three days. Nothin' for four or five days before that. Not since we left that bastard, Ben Stone."

"That ain't good, Logan," Mrs. Winn said.

"I know that ain't good," said Logan.

"Well, you bring me some water and soap and a towel or two and get out of my way. W, there's a night dress in the top of my trunk and a blue dress and things. You bring that in here and say good night. You can eat your supper on the porch."

The men brought what she'd asked for and went outside. Kane threw hay to the mules and began to curry the harness sweat from them. He listened to Mrs. Winn talking to Rachel Stone.

"Well, dear, you've been through a hard time, but now you're safe. It's time to get better now." She undressed Rachel and began to wash her. Her hands were gentle and life-giving as they touched the raw red scars on Rachel's desecrated body. "Sight, dear, you ain't been near water in some time." She worked over Rachel a long time.

"I don't want to get better," Rachel said softly. Kane heard her voice for the first time since leaving Stone's Crossing. He nearly looked through the door but caught himself and turned back to the mule's broad back.

"That's the devil talkin'," said Mrs. Winn, continuing her ministrations.

"They done vile things to me," Rachel said. "Bad things."

"You ain't the first," said Mrs. Winn. "And from history, you ain't likely the last. What can't be changed is best overcome and forgot. You pull yourself together and go on."

"Why?" asked Rachel. "What have I to live for? My husband denies me and has remarried. My children are dead."

"You are carrying a child," Lou Winn said.

Kane dropped the brush but did not stoop to get it.

"A red nigger child. How'd I even know whose it was?" Rachel spit out the words.

"Why, it's your child, that's whose it is," Mrs. Winn said softly. "And it's God's child."

Rachel said nothing. Kane retrieved the brush from the soft stall floor and continued brushing the mules.

"Now what's done is done. And you've been given a trust in this child. A child can make the world over for you. Logan and Silas Stone will always stand by you. So will W and I. Why, there's scads of folks ain't got a single good friend. And you've got four standin' shoulder to shoulder with you. You think this over, child. It's your good chance, girl. The Book says: overcome evil with good."

Kane did not see the faint smile flicker lightly across Rachel Stone's dry lips. Lou Winn did. She felt better about the woman. Lou finished tending Rachel and dressed her in her own best white cotton nightgown. She ladled stew from Logan's pot into a tin plate, cut a piece of his sugared cornbread, and poured a cup of the walking-strong coffee. She found a napkin and a spoon. Before going out, Lou sat the meal on the chair by the bed.

Kane heard the door close gently on its leather hinges.

65

He peaked in quickly at Rachel who sat on the side of the bed looking at the food. She sat a long time so Kane went away to hear the talk on the porch.

Lou Winn sat down in her oak rocker that W had brought from the wagon. "I think she will be all right," she said slowly. "She's thin, and she's been cruelly used, but she's strong underneath. Her bones are strong. Now her mind, I do not know about that. Seems like part of her ain't there, or maybe something that ain't normally there is in its place. I do not know."

"But she's goin' to make it?" asked Logan, hungry for assurance.

Mrs. Winn looked down at the man sitting at her feet on the first step. It was too dark in the shadows to see the question in her eyes. "Well, Jacob, she talked to me, and she sat up. I left her a mess of food. If she'll eat some, I think she's got a good chance."

Logan sat back against the step and looked out into the darkness. "Good," he said. "I knew a woman would make a difference."

"Logan and I talked about him going to tell Silas the news," W said. "The boy and I could finish the cabin. Now if you're a mind to, Lou, we could over-winter here."

Lou rocked. "That might be a useful thing," she said in the darkness.

Chapter Eight

The next morning, Rachel came to the cabin door and smelled the sweet, fresh, day-like bread baking in the oven. Her plate was empty when Lou picked it up. Rachel Stone had decided to live.

Kane carried wood for the wash pot fire the women built in the yard. Whenever women wanted to begin or start over, their first move was cleaning and washing. At least that was the conclusion the boy had reached.

Lou had a wagon half filled with lye soap, brooms, mop rags, and buckets. Before noon, she brushed out the cabin and mopped it on hands and knees. Logan's cabin had a floor which was a luxury on the frontier, and Lou Winn wanted to see it. She set bread to baking beside a couple of large dried apple pies in Dutch ovens.

Rachel was weak, but she tended the wash fire and helped Lou hang up the clothes she scrubbed clean on a wash board. Lines strung between the house and the wagon fluttered faded clothes on the wind. When clothes dried, Rachel took them down and sorted them for mending. They needed mending.

That morning, Lou Winn baked and cooked lunch, scrubbed the cabin, and washed the clothes of five people. When she had time, she brought water to the men as they worked on the addition to Logan's cabin. Lou commanded a kind of war against disorder with tactics, intelligence, and much intensity. She was here and then there, an unruffled general with shells exploding all around her.

In the afternoon, Lou showed Kane how to build a narrow pen and nest boxes in the lean-to. When it was ready, she set her chickens loose. When the clotheslines were empty of washed clothes, her quilts went out to air and color the breeze, prayers on the wind. And while all the work proceeded, Lou had time to check on Rachel, patting and encouraging, lifting the ragged woman from despair. Her blue dress was pretty on Rachel.

Lou Winn sat down at last to mend shirts and trousers worn ragged on the frontier. "Jacob," she called from the cabin door, "come in here a minute."

Logan put down his axe and went to her.

A roll of coarse cloth lay on the table along with her sewing things and a handful of weights to hold down her patterns. "I want to measure you for a new shirt. Daylight's showing through yours and the boy's shirts. You're a wearin' rags, Jacob."

Logan's newest old shirt was on the table. Lou picked it up and held it against him, measuring the shoulders against his lean back. She raised his arms and checked the length of a sleeve against his sweaty brown arms.

"Sit a minute, Jacob," Lou said when she finished.

"W will need me pretty quick," Logan said, sitting, elbows on legs, hands fidgeting between his knees.

Lou nodded. "This won't take long." Logan relaxed in the chair with Lou Winn standing in front of him, arms folded over his old shirt. "What are your feelin's about Rachel Stone?" she asked.

"Well," said Logan. "I don't know as I got feelin's about her, 'cept it ain't right what she's been through . . . first with the Indians, then with her own husband."

"That's all?" asked Lou.

"What more is there?" asked Logan in puzzlement.

68

"You ain't thinkin' she's dirt for being with the Indian bucks?"

"Well, what could she have done about that?" Logan asked.

"You ain't plannin' to keep her for your own pleasure?"

"I ain't," Logan said, shocked by Lou's thoughts. "Mercy, Lou."

"Jacob," Lou said, sitting on the bench, looking straight into his blue eyes, "do you care for Rachel?"

Logan stood up. "Well, of course, I care for her. I been through a lot of trouble finding and delivering that woman. She are admirable for courage, too, livin' through what no man could of stood."

Lou sat back. "It's as I thought."

"Now hold on here, Lou," Logan said. "I ain't likin' your direction. That woman ain't nothin' to me more than a common, decent concern. I ain't touched her. And I ain't lusted after her neither."

"Of course, you ain't, Jacob," said Lou quietly. "You love her. And you've took her to yourself."

Logan stood amazed, stupefied. "Lou," he said, "I ain't thought such thoughts."

"Ain't the thoughts, Jacob. It's the doin', the little kindnesses," the woman said.

"I swear," Logan said and sat down. "I ain't touched her in no forward way."

"Now listen here, Jacob," Lou said, "I've known you a long time, since we all come to Texas. You ain't near as hard as you act to be. You ain't facile about women or love. You're easy hurt."

Logan sat in the chair with his hands between his knees. "Lou, I wish you'd stop this. I ain't a bit comfortable with such personal talk. I'm needed outside."

69

"Jacob," Lou said putting her hand on his arm. "Rachel Stone is carrying a child . . . an Indian child she believes."

Logan didn't move or speak for a full minute. He just looked out the open door at the prairie. "That's the way of it," he said finally. "I got to help W now, Lou."

The woman walked to the door with Logan. Before he went out, she said very softly, "You needed to know, Jacob, for your plannin'."

Logan looked down at the little woman. His outstretched fingers pushed a fall of hair back from his eyes. "You meant it for my good, I know that," he said, and went out.

Logan picked up his axe in the yard and sent the tension from his mind and body down the smooth handle through the iron head into the log he had left. He continued to work after the others went in to supper. Lou Winn sat a plate aside for him — covered it with a white napkin.

After supper, Kane found the frontiersman sitting on the creek bank watching the last light leave the land. He sat down beside Logan. "Missus Wynn has washed your things and packed some food for your journey," he said.

"I got everything I need, then?" asked Logan.

"I guess," said Kane.

"I'll tell Silas Stone we got Rachel. She really is Rachel, I'll say. She is alive sure enough up here. She's here 'cause Ben wouldn't recognize her and has a new wife. I can't get too colorful. Just tell it plain," Logan said.

"Why don't you write this down, Logan? Send a letter?" Kane asked.

"These are things best said to a man," said Logan.

"What do you want Silas Stone to do about Rachel?" the boy asked.

"I want him to do whatever he thinks best. She can live here. This ain't no bad place. Or we'll carry her wherever he wants her to go," Logan said.

Kane suddenly had a thought. "Logan, are you going to marry Rachel Stone?"

"I'll do what's right by her," the man said quietly. "I figure she's free. Silas may see it different. We'll see what he says. More important, we'll see what she says."

"You know about the baby?" asked the boy.

"I know," said the man.

"That doesn't make any difference?" asked the boy.

"The needs the greater," said the man. He turned to Kane. "Look, Kane, this ain't no storybook. I ain't the handsome prince. I'm a man who's traveled here and there. I done plenty of wild things. I wouldn't mind to settle down. I believe I could make a good life for a woman and a child. I'm a solid worker. Don't drink to speak of." Kane dropped his head. "You ain't so little you hate an unborn child 'cause it's an Indian, are you, boy?" Logan asked.

"Ain't me, Logan," said the boy. "You saw the folks at Stone's Crossing."

"That's a fact," the man said. "What chance has that baby got without me? It ain't got no chance at all. Unborn and already no chance at all. That ain't right, Kane. I never hated Indians like some. They are just people same as us. Some of 'em I like better than us. They are part of this land, part of me and you now. In a way, I couldn't have no better child, so much more a part of the country even than I am.

71

I sure ain't going to hold hate against no baby."

"You are a good man, Logan," Kane said, knowing now more what a good man was.

"I ain't good, son. I just got a chance here to do one little thing right, that's all," Logan said. "Now, come daylight, I'll ride out for San Antone. Somebody there will know where Silas Stone is. You're plenty good enough to take care of things here. You and W will have the cabin up 'fore I can get back." The man stopped. "Don't you take off now while I'm gone. I made your pa a promise to see you through. And I aim to do it. Besides I'd miss you and your drawing books."

Chapter Nine

At noon, Kane handed Sarai a piece of jerked meat and settled back against the sunny side of an old pecan tree. He chewed thoughtfully. Sarai dipped a gourd from her bag into the small stream. Ripples spread around the broken surface and slowly disappeared.

"I've got fish hooks," said Rachel to the boy on the creek bank.

She came down beside him on the grassy place. Pulling the hooks from her pocket, she displayed them on the palm of her hand. Kane saw the fresh healing scars on her wrists where her captors' rawhide ropes cut deeply into the thin flesh.

"These are thorns," she said of the hooks she held. "I picked them off a bush myself in Sonora. Every bush and tree there is covered with stickers and thorns. Various sizes of hooks . . . little to big . . . grow on the same shrub. As you see there are several strong beards on each. Why these hooks are quite as strong as any made of steel and are more elastic. Test it yourself."

She offered the hooks in her palms to the boy. He carefully lifted a thorn. Kane tried the sharpness of the point and the flex under Rachel's interested eyes.

"Why that is something, Miss Rachel," he said, looking into her face. The baby had made her face fuller and softer someway. "It's a curiosity."

"Oh, it's much more than a curiosity. I have caught myself many a fish supper on these very thorn hooks,"

Rachel said. "Comanches don't eat fish so I had 'em all to myself. A person should never starve who possessed such serviceable hooks. Let us fish ourselves a supper."

They fished away the Sunday afternoon and talked of the places Rachel had seen with the nomadic Kiowas of Bull Back's band. Lou and W came down and sat with them. That evening, after W and Kane cleaned the fish, Lou rolled them in egg, flour, and corn meal and fried them crisp over the fire. They ate fish and spoon bread and sat back contented to listen to Rachel's stories of the far West.

"You must go there one day," she said. "And stand as I have stood on a pinnacle of a mountain and see one mountain beyond another until they are lost in the misty air. It is a dreadful rough range of mountains. I suppose it is as high as any others in the world. The bottoms are very rich. It will be winter on top of the mountains, and spring or summer in the valleys. Where you can see the valleys, you will often see them covered with the buffalo, sometimes with the elk, the wild horses." She sat quietly seeing the vistas again.

"You should write down your story, Rachel," Lou Winn said.

"Would be a help to folks," W added. "I reckon you have seen places and things most folks ain't seen, won't see for fifty year maybe."

Rachel thought about their proposal. "It is true I have seen the far places . . . beautiful and curious places, places that will one day make rich farms and pastures. Still I am better at the telling than the writing down. My thoughts go flat when I pick up pen and paper."

"I could write down for you," Kane said. He suddenly wanted to hear, to record, to preserve, not just the stories

74

but Rachel Stone — before she disappeared like the morning fog along the creek bottom.

"I'd spell you when you were tired," said Lou. "If you'd help me with the hard spelling."

"Well, then," said Rachel, "I will tell you what I have seen with my eyes and know for fact to be true. We shall pass the winter, most agreeably."

"Is there not a tablet of paper in our old trunk, W?" asked Lou.

"Aye, there is," said W. "And a journal, too. Saved for the day we had something unusual to write down."

The writing sessions began in the evenings after supper. Kane sat at the table Lou had wiped clean and laid out with the paper, a bottle of India ink, and a steel nibbed pen. Rachel talked of animals — beasts, she called them — beaver, antelope, bear, buffalo.

" 'But ask, now, the beast, and they shall teach thee; and the fowls of the air, and they shall tell thee. Or speak to the earth, and it shall teach thee; and the fishes of the sea shall declare unto thee. Who knoweth not in all these that the hand of the Lord hath wrought this? In whose hand is the soul of every living thing, and the breath of all mankind.' Job said that in his hard times," Rachel began.

There were places in Rachel's words. The salt plains lay where the eternal wind blew milky crystals into knee deep drifts. Sonora waited where every bush and tree bore thorns and curious springs gurgled forth a yellow tar that burned like whale oil.

There were Rachel's discoveries, too — the prairies as level as the surface of lakes because, she said, they had once been lakes, no, a great sea. The sea shells, oysters and such, found about or imbedded in stone proved it to Rachel. Once she said, she discovered shining

75

*particles, three quarters of an inch around, oblong, per-
fectly transparent. They gave her light to work by and
disclosed the ravine where they lay from a mile's distance.
Diamonds, she thought the glowing particles were, to
go with the gold the Indians found and made into arrow
points. It was a pity, Rachel said, that such wealth
remained undiscovered in that lost valley, but one day
it should be one of the richest mines ever discovered.
Perhaps the man who would own it was not yet born.
And yet it waited through all time for him.*

Chapter Ten

Kane and the woman, Sarai, made a late camp at the end of the day's ride. Kane built a small fire and cooked. Sarai heated water in a small copper bowl and washed small portions of the baby. She powdered her with the pale dust of a rotten log. The child giggled contentedly on the spread bed roll and ate her supper. When the meal was over, Kane rolled out the other blankets he had brought from the horses hidden in a thicket down the creek.

"Come here," he said in Comanche. "You sleep here."

Sarai came to where he squatted on the blankets. Kane fastened an iron cuff around her ankle and then around his own. He watched her soft mouth set.

"Don't like that, huh?" he muttered to himself. "Well, I don't either. But I intend to get some sleep, and I cannot if I spend the night worrying about you changing your mind and taking off. Go to sleep."

Kane lay back on his own blanket. The woman moved her saddle and blanket as far from him as the chain allowed and sat down on it.

"I sure hope it doesn't come a norther tonight," he said then. "You'd freeze." He thought a moment. "Maybe not."

Kane sat by the small fire looking at Sarai's back. At last he reached across her for his own saddle bags. Sarai turned quickly at his weight and watched him warily as he sat back up.

"Just getting something I want to look at," Kane said.

"What?" the woman asked.

"Rachel's journal," he said. "I found it among my old things in Belknap. I wanted to see it again. Look. Here's a sketch I made of Rachel. Do you remember your aunt?"

Sarai looked at the line drawing softly modeled with cross-hatchings. "She was taken away," she said.

"Where?" asked Kane.

"Away," Sarai said. Reading Kane's face, she continued, "to the Kiowas."

"Then what?"

"I do not know," Sarai said. "I never saw her again."

"Did you cry when she was taken?" Kane asked.

"No."

"Why not?" the man asked. "Do you remember anything honestly now that you are a Comanche?"

Sarai looked at the ground, then through hooded eyes she looked into Kane's face. "The raiders killed the children who cried too much. We did not cry any more."

"Do you know what Rachel went through?" Kane asked harshly, angry at Sarai for not knowing or caring more about Rachel, for being white yet so thoroughly Comanche."

"The men tore at Rachel and the other woman. We saw their white legs. Their private parts. They screamed and cried." Sarai seemed to be listening intently as she spoke. "They were just meat for the men, but they were still alive. Their protest and pain stimulated the men."

Kane said nothing. Sarai looked into the fire; then she lay back resting against the bags and saddle. Her fingers touched Summer's dark hair, smoothed it.

"Rachel had children," Kane said.

"Tehan," said Sarai.

"Jamie. Jamie, that's his white name," Kane said. "He's an Indian now sure as hell . . . worse than an Indian from what I know."

"Worse," Sarai agreed. "*White* Indian."

Kane grabbed Sarai's arm, lifting her away from the rest. "Here's what your precious Indians did to Rachel's baby." He released Sarai roughly, opened the journal and began to read. "I wrote this down myself."

"In the early summer, I gave birth to my second son. He was very small and seemed to me old and wizen when I looked into his little face. There was no help for us. No women offered me care or kindness. The poor baby was born into my own hands and wrapped in the filthy garments I wore. The cup of my sorrow among my captors had reached the brim and was soon to overflow.

"My owner resented the child as I was not able to labor as well as before. One morning five or six large Indians came to me. As soon as they came into the empty, silent teepee, I felt my heart sick; fears agitated my whole frame almost to convulsion; my body shook with fear. I knew my helplessness before them."

Rachel spoke evenly without emotion, a spectator at her own misery.

"One of them caught hold of the child by the throat. Like a lion holding its prey, all intensity and power concentrated in the killing hold, triumphant yet steady in its power of death, he held the child with all his strength crushing out the life until the poor creature appeared entirely dead.

"How feeble I was to save the poor creature. They laughed at me as I fought them. My struggle excited

79

their worst nature and my pain gave them new delight in a horrible game. They began to throw the child's body about, keeping him away from me, throwing him into the air and letting him fall against the hard earth.

"When they grew tired, they gave him back to me. I had no tears left. I merely sat looking at the bruised body. But he yet lived. I washed the blood from his face. That he might live! That he might live. My hope, my fear, my anguish grew.

"But they watched. They saw. They had not gone. Brazenly they stole my hope. Arrogant before the powers of kindness, they took my hope and broke it on the earth.

"They jerked the baby from my hands and tied a plaited rope around his bruised neck. They pulled it hard and tight. They threw the baby into a ledge of prickly pears which was eight to twelve feet high. Then, they pulled his tender flesh down, down through the tearing spines. Such a soundless, soft cry it gave . . . so soft. Many times, throwing, pulling through.

"I watched, quiet now, nothing to do but watch. One got a horse and tied the rope to his saddle. He rode, like Achilles with Hector, in a great circle dragging the child behind the horse until it was not only lifeless, but torn to shreds. At last he stopped, picked it up by the leg, and threw it at me like a rabbit to skin.

"In praise of my captors, they gave me time to dig a small hole and bury the remains. As I patted the dirt into a mound and lay heavy stones on top, my heart filled with joy. My now happy infant was beyond them. I rejoiced that it had passed from this place of suffering and sorrow.

"You cannot come to me; but I must come to you. 'Praise God with whom the innocents dwell safely forever. Oh, Dear Savior, bring me to dwell in the sweet realm of endless bliss with my sweet babes forever.' To die is gain.

"After that, I determined to make them kill me. When Bull Back's daughter shoved me, I rose up and beat her with a stick of fire wood.

" 'Damn you,' I said. 'Damn you all to hell.'

"Her mother cried out.

" 'Scream,' I said. 'Will do you no better good than it did me.'

"I beat on the daughter, hitting her hard, again and again, until I saw her face, her eyes. I quit then, threw the stick away.

"They did not kill me . . . they accepted me. I counted that another cruelty."

"Go to sleep," Kane said gently.

Chapter Eleven

The sliver of moon lingered near the horizon casting a faint shadow of light across the prairie night. Sarai's hand closed over Kane's mouth. He opened his eyes, but saw her finger gesture silence against her lips. She spoke in Spanish: "Riders coming."

"I know," he said softly. He turned back the blanket and sat up. "Gather your things. We'll go down the wash toward the horses."

Sarai quickly picked up her child and the blankets they slept on. Kane tossed her his blankets, gathered the saddles and bags and the rifle.

"Let's go."

The chain still binding them to each other, they slipped over the side and into the wash just before the riders rode in. Kane motioned for the woman to lie down against the near wall of the dirt bank under the slight overhang. He lay down beside her. They listened to the noise of the men kicking through the camp. Kane rolled over her body as the voices came near the edge of the draw. They waited, listening.

The voices lingered, debated, quarreled. The raiders left the edge, returned to eat what was left of the last night's supper from a pan near the embers of the fire.

"Why don't you call out?" Kane whispered against Sarai's ear.

"I do not desire your death, Kane," the woman whispered back.

The raiders above finished their meal. At last, they went away.

Even after a long wait, Kane did not move off Sarai. He liked the closeness of the woman. He wanted to run his hand along her hip and leg, but did not. Still he did not move.

Sarai twisted, restless to be released.

"They are gone," she said.

Without thinking, Kane suddenly kissed her, holding her, enjoying it. She did not return the kiss, but pushed against him.

"Yes, Miss Sarai," he said reluctantly. "We're moving out."

Kane lifted the woman and child from the sand. Without thought, he dusted the sand from Sarai's back. She flared.

"Oh, settle down," he said.

Kane considered the logistics. He took the saddles and rifle, leaving the woman to struggle with the child, blankets, and bags.

"That's the Comanche way, isn't it?" he asked as they walked slowly along the wash toward the horses. The chain between them dragged and caught. Each time Sarai bent, set down her load, and pulled it free.

"Catch up the leads," Kane said, when they reached the horses.

Sarai struggled to get the ropes. Kane swung the saddles up and tightened the girds loosely. He took the child.

"Come on, come on," he said as the woman re-gathered herself. "We'll walk a while down this defile."

They walked till well after daylight before Kane stopped, sat the baby on the ground, and began to tighten the saddle girds for riding. Sarai dropped her bundles. She jerked the chain.

"Off," she said in English.

"Off?" Kane said innocently, but he kneeled to unlock the cuffs. He removed his first. "Why, Miss Sarai, you're wet." He touched the wet stain the baby had made on her skirt as they lay in the draw. Sarai struck his hand.

Sarai was angry. She kicked sand at him. And then, the words, in Spanish, began to tumble out, fast and dirty, "You think I spread my legs for you, you puffed up bull calf? You could not run that many miles, buffalo calf." She kicked more sand.

Kane caught the allusion. During the buffalo rut, bulls, sometimes five or six, chased a cow for miles until the exhausted fell away and only the strongest bull remained to mate the cow.

"I don't know," he shot back. "I've run about twenty-five years after you so far." He studied her. "Hell, it was only a kiss. A spur of the moment impulse, being close and all. Don't make so much of it. I'm not after you."

His words made her angrier.

"Stupid," she flared, kicking more sand. "Stupid campfire, stupid camp. Stupid! You are very lucky those Indians were in a hurry to go somewhere else. Lucky I did not call out. Stupid! You get me and child killed! Stupid!"

Kane began to enjoy her anger. The blue eyes flashed. She involved him, talked to him. He laughed with pleasure. She became more angry. "Let's get that wet skirt off," he teased, reaching for the waist again. She pushed his hand away. "That must be what's got you so stirred up . . . being wet and uncomfortable and all. Walking didn't help much either, I guess." Then Kane quit joking,

84

"Believe me, lady, I wouldn't touch you without a formal invitation if you were stark naked."

"Good," she said.

Sarai turned and moved away toward her pony. She lifted Summer onto the saddle and put her foot into the stirrup. Kane looked at the line of her, lean and supple. He cocked his head slightly and shook it.

"I thought Indian women were always willing. Never spoke hard words to a man, never said no," Kane said innocently, unwilling to give up the contest, the contact.

Sarai stepped down, turned, and placed her hands on her hips. She walked into Kane, forcing him backward.

"You thought! You don't think too good so far. Your scalp could be riding down to Mexico right now, *gringo.* You'd better think about your thinking."

Kane looked at the open face before him. He wanted to hold her, but knew he could not. She would not have it, and he would not force it.

"So you've had about enough of us white folks pushing and prodding," Kane said, mostly to himself. "I wish it were that easy. But you haven't met Ben Stone, not yet. Ben sure changed things for the worse for Rachel."

Chapter Twelve

Ben Stone did not sweat under his black coat and broad-brimmed, flat-crowned hat in the late spring sun. He rode a fine horse into the yard at Logan's cabin.

"I have come at my father's request," he said to Logan who stood on the cabin porch. "You have carried hard words against me, Jacob Logan. We will set this straight between us before I leave."

"How are you? Nice day, ain't it, too?" said Logan.

"I've ridden a long way," said Stone.

"We've all ridden a long way," said Logan, stepping up and resting his foot on the hitch rail. "Most of it uphill."

"You'll not ask me down or inside?" asked Stone.

"No, I won't," Logan said. "The matter is settled, and I don't aim to stir it again. You have a nice trip home."

"You say she is my wife . . . an accusation."

"I don't say she's your wife any more. She is Rachel Stone," said Logan. "She's free and independent of you and all that you are."

"Let me look upon her," Stone said.

"No," said Logan. "She ain't a gazing stock. You saw her at Stone's Crossing. She's exactly the same woman as she was then."

"You've taken her up?" asked Stone.

"I've taken her up," said Logan.

"You sin against me," said Stone.

"You lyin', sin-sayin' hypocrite, get the hell off

my place," Logan said.

"As you drive me off my own property with lies to my father?" asked Ben.

"So there's more to it, Stone. There's money in here somewhere, ain't there? You ain't here for Rachel's sake. You are here for something else. What is it, snake?"

"You've set up against me . . . you and my own father. My land is tied up, and I want it released. I have a buyer for property deeded to Rachel Stone. She must sign the paper."

Logan smiled and kicked at splinters on the porch. "Son-of-a-gun, Stone, we've found your heart at last. Rachel owns whatever she owns by a gift from Silas Stone. It ain't yours to sell. Enjoy your ride back."

"I will talk to Rachel," said Ben Stone.

"To whom?" asked Logan.

"You damn well know to whom," Stone said.

"Who do you want here?" Logan pursued.

"Rachel Stone," Stone said. Then an idea hit him. "Rachel Stone, come forth." He commanded this to the cabin door behind Logan.

"Stay put, Rachel. This . . . ," Logan searched for a word bad enough, low enough for Stone, "this piece of shit is leaving."

The cabin door scraped across the boards and slowly opened. Rachel came out. Logan turned.

"Rachel, you don't have to do anything he says. He ain't over you in any way."

Rachel stood beside Logan, looking at Stone.

"Who is he?" she asked Logan. "I don't rightly know this man."

"You know me," Stone said between his teeth. "You know me very well, woman."

"I'm sorry, stranger," Rachel said. "But I don't recall.

87

You must be in error. We've never met."

Ben Stone's anger ran down through his legs and out into the horse. It faunched and turned under him. He fought it back to the front.

"This isn't a game. It's money. Sign this paper."

He pulled a thick fold of papers from his coat.

"You'll get a fair portion minus the fees and handling, of course."

"She'll get it all," said Logan. "Or she won't sign nothing."

"Damn you for interfering," said Stone, fighting the horse. "Damn you in your adulterous life. Damn the lot of you. Cursed be your life from this moment forward."

Logan felt Rachel starting to shiver against him. He put his arm around her and the baby.

"Filth and offal of savages," Stone spat out. "Unfit you are for a decent home or life. Live on the prairie with the heathen, seek out the savage passion. No white man will ever touch you. You're damned, Rachel. I damn you, Rachel. Damned is that red whelp that nurses where my dead son nursed. God will never forgive you for what you've done to me this day."

The curses cut into Logan. He felt Rachel slipping away, disappearing into the morning fog, beyond his reach.

"You ain't got one right to damn anybody. Your own curses come back at you, Stone. I turn 'em like a mirror back at you." Seeing Rachel's white face, Logan reached for the rifle propped against the porch post. "I've decided to kill you. That's all there is to it. It's over for me, Stone. You are a dead man."

Logan raised the rifle and sighted on Stone's forehead. Their eyes met over the long barrel. Stone spun the horse. The shot echoed through the still air and dust.

Ben Stone was gone.

"Rachel," Logan said, but Rachel had turned away.

The days passed at the cabin on the frontier. None of them spoke of Ben Stone, but his words and presence were a heavy burden on their hearts. A world of bitter darkness clouded their lives.

"How can anybody do something like that? Doesn't he see the hurt of it?" the boy asked Lou. "It's like he's ruined everything, every chance for happiness, burned every bridge for Rachel . . . nothing here, no forgiveness later. Just nothing. She takes such things seriously."

"I expect," said Lou, as Kane sat stabbing his knife into the dirt, "I expect that man will take some getting over. But it's not right what he said. It's not right. And it's not right for us to give in to his thoughts. We've got to hold good thoughts of love and hope. Think on these things that are good and just and true and lovely and of good report. Hold on hard and fast, right now."

The boy looked up. "How?"

Lou Wynn came down and sat on the step beside him.

"Kane, the world is full of right and wrong and joy and hurt and sorrow. Justice is a rare thing. Love is a rare thing. But they are real . . . like cardinals are real and rare in a world full of sparrows. But you look out for 'em, and you know 'em, and you smile when one comes suddenly into a tree before you.

"Sometime in your own life, you have to decide what you are going to hold to, hold out for. W and I decided a long time ago we were going to live toward God's good way."

"Ben Stone thinks he's God's own man . . . able

89

to curse folks for God," Kane said.

"He doesn't bear good fruit, son. The Master said there would be many false teachers but to judge them by their fruit. Ben Stone didn't bring any love or joy or kindness or gentleness or goodness . . . did he? That's the fruit of the Spirit of God. . . ."

"He thinks he's right."

"Doesn't matter what he thinks. Matters what you think, how you choose to live. You going to let him choose for you by dragging around bad thoughts, bad as his own?"

The boy sat still. "Lou, why can't we just hate Ben Stone?"

The woman smiled softly. " 'Cause it will do him no harm and us no good. Let's go hoe us some weeds." She patted his arm as they walked toward the garden.

"Where's Rachel?" asked Logan as he came in with fresh venison tied across his saddle.

"She's in the cabin," said Lou, barely looking up from her digging. Logan rode on to the house.

Kane stood up and stretched his long back. "I believe I'll get a drink," he said.

"Go on," said Lou as she sat back on her heels in the loose soil. She wiped the sweat from her forehead with the nearly clean back of her hand. "I could stand a dipper full myself."

Before she stood, she watched Logan hang the deer carcass for dressing from the pecan tree. He led his horse to the porch and leaned his rifle against the post. Kane sat on the step beside the water bucket drinking the cool spring water.

"What's that, Logan?" the boy asked.

Logan stopped, stood, listening.

The sound came again from Rachel's cabin. It was a soft gritty sound, like sticking something sharp into a bag of grain or flour. Not loud, just soft and solid, in, out, in, out. And then, Rachel's screams, mad, mournful screams, filled the air.

The dipper fell from Kane's hand. Logan reached for the gun, a frontiersman's reflex. Before Kane could get to his feet, Logan broke through the locked cabin door. Kane came behind him.

Rachel, covered in blood, blood flowing from deep gashes cut across her wrists, sat on the hearth, sticking a knife in and out of the dead baby. Kane saw it, saw the insane look in Rachel's eyes as she looked up smiling, wiping the baby's blood with her own across her face with one hand, plunging the knife into the child with the other.

Kane saw Logan's rifle come up, saw him sight, saw his finger draw back the brass trigger, saw the hammer move, saw the black smoke come out and fill the room, saw Rachel slam back and slump against the fireplace, and slowly fall over the dead baby. Her hand released the knife, and it fell on the stones.

"Dear God in heaven," Lou said behind them. "W, oh, W, come here quick!"

Logan stood, still holding the rifle in firing position. He stood fixed as they waited.

"W!" Lou said, her shaking hands, grabbing for her husband as he came to the door. W caught her and folded her hands inside his own.

Logan lowered the gun slowly, and carefully leaned it against the wall. He went to Rachel and the baby.

"I love you, Rachel," he said, sitting beside her, wiping the hair from her blood-and-tear-streaked face. "I would have done right by you, both of you, all my life."

Logan touched young Jacob and rested his head against the cool stones of the fireplace. Tears ran silently out of his faded eyes, down the brown cheeks, down to his mouth and jaw. He held the dead woman and her dead baby.

Kane leaned against the cabin wall. He'd never been sick like this — so sick there was nothing left in him. Lou and W stood near him, watching Logan, hearing his sobs.

Finally, Lou came slowly into the acrid, smoke-filled cabin. She walked to Logan. Offering her hand, she said gently, "Come on now, Jacob. Come with me."

Logan looked up at her sweet face.

"I can't leave Rachel and the baby."

Lou kneeled beside Logan, touched his forehead with her lips.

"You've done all that can be done for them, Jacob. Take my hand now."

Logan looked at Rachel, the baby; then he took Lou's hand, and gently released the dead woman and child. Lou led him out of the cabin to the stone steps.

"Sit right here, Jacob."

Lou sat beside him, holding his hand. They sat like that past noon — Logan silently weeping, Lou holding his callused, bloody hand.

Kane did not really hear the first shot. The reins and lead line in his hand jerked, and he looked up at the vast emptiness around him. He vaulted into the saddle without thought before the second shot.

"Where did that come from?" he asked Sarai in Comanche.

She gestured toward a low hill.

"Hell's bells!"

Kane jerked her horse around with the lead line. Leaning low over the horses, he and the woman rode toward a water-cut draw. Dirt kicked up where shots hit around them. They slid down the eroded side of the cut. The defile was deep enough that they did not have to dismount, but sat in their saddles as more shots peppered the rim of the wash.

"Who in hell?" Kane said, trying to analyze the shooting. He stood up in his stirrups, craning to see beyond the draw, to catch sight of the shooter. A bullet kicked dirt in his face. He sat quickly back.

Sarai looked up and down the deep cut in the land. She touched Kane's hand and pointed toward a curve in the cut.

"Come on, then," he said, towing the woman and her horse behind him along the wash. "I'd like to know who that is. But right now I just don't want to be where he thinks I am. Your Comanches would be on us in a swarm by now," he muttered to himself. "It is not Indians, unless it's just one or two maybe. Wonder where that damn Caleb Matthews got off to? Did he have a big bore repeater? Who else even knows we're out here? Hell's bells, everybody! . . . every Indian-hatin', pea brained body."

Kane's mind sorted the possibilities. An unpleasant thought hit him.

"No," he said softly. "Not Logan."

Chapter Thirteen

"Logan?" asked the young chain bearer, Ramsey. "Do you see that Indian?"

"I see him," Logan said. "Stay where you are. If something starts, head for the wagons."

The Indian rode slowly off the fold in the earth and down toward the surveying party. He was tall and sat the horse as comfortably, as essentially, as if he were part of it, as only a Comanche could. The pony he rode was small, spotted, sharp and responsive to commands that other men never saw.

The man's clothes were beaded buckskin, a light buff color, with fringes a foot long. The moccasins on his feet trailed fur and leather fringes almost to the ground. His hair was drawn into three braids — a scalp lock that hung indolently over his copper forehead, and the side braids, wrapped in otter fur and red wool. Gold and silver and shell earrings hung from the edges of his ears.

The set of the mouth, the look of the eyes, the weathering of his skin showed that this Indian was a seasoned warrior. He was not young. But this one would never be old if he lived to be one hundred. There was intelligence and vitality — life force — in him. A long white scar ran across the high cheek bone under his right eye, permanently ornamenting his face. Behind him came another warrior, covering his back, but not close, two or three horse-lengths away.

The party of surveyors Logan led watched the Indian,

forgetting about the beans and bacon lunch getting cold in their tin plates. They did not even chew the food already in their mouths. A quick count showed there were ten of the men, only two Indians. The surveyors were generally well-armed, but their guns were stacked against the wagons. Some had even left their sidearms behind when they washed for lunch. Their quick glances led the Indian to observe the indolent rifles — nearby, but perhaps a lifetime away.

The surveyors, locators, and chainbearers, cook and fetcher, searched the Indian, checking his armaments. A gun rested across his thighs, hidden in the soft, long-fringed and beaded leather scabbard. The white men hoped it was an old single shot front stuffer. It was not. The Indian had a new repeater, as good as any they had. The second one did, too.

The Comanche reined up, almost on top of Logan.

"Is that the eye of God?" asked the Indian.

Logan dropped his hand on top of the transit.

"It don't see quite that much," said Logan.

"But it sees enough to take away our land," the Comanche said.

"Maybe so," Logan said. He reached into his pocket and pulled out a little cloth bag of tobacco with cigarette papers. "Smoke?"

The Indian took it — opened the sack, placed the papers, sprinkled amber tobacco on the thin papers held in his long fingers. Looking at Logan, he licked and rolled the cigarette, then handed the bag and papers back. He waited for Logan to roll his smoke. Logan struck a sulphur match. The warrior leaned into his face as he lit the cigarette. Their eyes met.

"Nobah," Logan said.

"Lo-gan," the Comanche said, and sat up. He looked

around as he smoked. Finally, he and the warrior with him rode slowly past the wagons with the stacked guns and through the camp. Logan, as still as the rocks above him, watched them go. He glanced around expecting to see Ramsey, but the boy was gone. The roll of earth where Nobah had sat above the camp was now lined with armed and painted warriors. Logan looked at his men — slack, relaxed with their dinner plates still in their hands. Nobah and his companion were gone. The draw where they disappeared was now lipped with more armed and painted warriors. Logan felt the bristly hairs rise on his leathery, tanned neck.

"Get your guns," he said as he walked with studied slowness toward the camp.

One of the surveyors threw down his plate and started to run toward a little ravine to the right side of the camp. Warriors appeared. A single shot caught the runner in full stride, lifting him before letting him fall to earth.

"Get the hell goin'," Logan said as the surveyors flew toward their guns and the scant protection of the wagons.

Logan had his pistol almost out when the first Comanche lancer pounded against him with the shoulder of his horse. Logan hit the ground. The gun flew out of his hand beneath the horse's hoofs. Logan swore. A shot hit the lancer. He pitched forward off the horse landing dead at Logan's side.

"Good shot," said Logan, stretching toward his gun.

Logan was on his hands and knees like a big spider scrambling over the prairie. A fusillade of fire broke out toward the surveyors. Logan saw two men fall. A puff of smoke from one of the wagons showed that one of his men got off a return shot. Logan crawled without grace or precaution, butt in the air, trying for the gun.

A pair of Comanches cantered toward him from behind.

"Hell," Logan said, hearing the hoofbeats, reaching for the gun. Logan had it. He turned, rolled on his back ready to fire. He pulled the trigger. The cylinder fell away. Logan began crawling backward on his hands and heels. He flipped and rose to run.

As fire from the hills and gullies pinned the surveyors in their wagons, the two Comanche warriors swung low between their galloping ponies and caught Logan under the arms. They lifted him kicking from the earth. They ran the ponies through the camp across the fire, dragging Logan's feet through the flames.

"Damn," Logan winced.

Past the wagons the Comanches circled with Logan — lifting, dragging, pulling the big Texian along toward the crest of the rise. Logan saw the boy, Ramsey, on his knees, a Comanche lance touching his neck. The warriors dropped Logan running beside the boy.

Warriors parted and Nobah appeared on the rise.

"Watch, Lo-gan," he said.

Logan's eyes turned from the Indian to his little camp. Comanche warriors sped past the wagons, ripping at the covers, untouched by the shots of his men. A warrior snatched a brand from the scattered fire.

"Shoot him, you sons-a-bitches," Logan swore. "Fight 'em, damn you."

A shot cracked, but left the Indian untouched. He rode against the wagon, touched the fire to the sheet. Dry as tinder, it caught, flamed. The Comanche whirled away toward the second wagon. He leaned forward with the brand. A rifle barrel met his naked belly. Logan

97

saw the black smoke bellow and the flesh of the warrior's middle blown away.

"Yeah. That's it," he shouted. But the flames were already rising on the second wagon.

The surveyors began to pour out, leaping off the wagon beds, heading for the small grove of trees down the ravine on the right. One man's shirt trailed fire as he ran. A warrior beside Nobah raised his rifle and dropped the man. One by one the Comanches picked the men off. One stood, the last, hands raised, backing toward the trees. A warrior rode off the hill. His shrill scream rose through the air. He hit the last surveyor full force with his lance, driving through his chest, pinning him limp to the tree.

The fighting tension left Logan's shoulders. He relaxed. They were all dead — all except him and the boy. The smoke from the wagons and guns shifted with the breeze blowing into Logan's eyes and nose. Water ran from his eyes over his sooty face. Logan spat.

"Damn you, Nobah," he said, starting toward the chief. A lancer raised his point against Logan's chest. Logan pushed on, piercing his own skin with the point. "Kill me or get the hell out of my way."

Before he could grab Nobah, several warriors slipped off their ponies and caught Logan. They wrestled him, trying to get him to the ground. He swung his fists with jaw crunching force. At last, they had him face down, spitting dust and grass.

"Sons-a-bitches," Logan said. "Let's make this a fair fight, me and him."

In moments, Logan was trussed up. A lance across his back, arms bound over the lance and tied securely in front with rawhide ropes. They stood him before

Nobah. He dropped a noose over Logan's head and jerked it tight.

"Ahe," the Comanche said. "You are mine, Quick-to-See. You are my dog until I have the woman again."

He kicked Logan in the chest, knocking him backward over his bound arms. At the same time he held the neck-rope tighter. Logan strangled and choked.

One of Nobah's warriors lifted the shaking Ramsey boy to his feet and drew him toward Nobah. The Indian looked down on the colorless boy. The boy's pale blue eyes squinted out from under white eyelashes, blinded by the sun behind the leader. Logan lay on his back with the rope tight on his neck.

Nobah spoke to Logan in Comanche: "Tell him, go tell what he has seen. Tell Kane: Logan for the woman." He jerked Logan's rope.

Logan's words strangled out. "Go on, boy," he said to the kid. "You can tell 'em that Nobah wants the woman back. Says he'll trade me for her. But you just get back the best you can. More than likely I am dead anyways. It's his play from here on. Get."

A Comanche warrior standing above the boy pushed him with his foot. The boy tumbled down the hill toward the camp of dead men. He hit on his feet at the bottom and began to run. Two warriors rode full gallop after him, lances fixed, shoulder to shoulder, screaming the Comanche war cry. Just before the lances touched him, the riders split off and circled back and slowed into a trot.

Chapter Fourteen

Silas Stone saw the two riders coming across the long prairie from the west. Most of the morning they were just dots moving on the yellow winter grass, disappearing and reappearing as the land opened before them. Silas was a man who could wait. He had waited since first light. He had waited since San Jacinto.

News of the recapture of Sarai had sent Silas into a flurry of preparations. He wanted a room fixed up. He wanted food, her special food, cooked. He looked at his house and saw its emptiness, even with his son, Ben, and his second wife, Jane, living there. Silas wanted flowers. He wanted the laughter he missed.

He wanted back his wife's smile, her touch on the house making it more than clean, making it beautiful by mingling native and natural things with the cherry wood table and the china she had brought from the old country, making it home. But Julia was long dead. Jane had known her, but was afraid she could not match the dead woman's homey gifts, and so Jane never tried to make Silas's home hers. She just cleaned and cooked and kept herself a servant.

Ben, Silas's living son, was bitter against bringing a savage — he called Sarai a savage — into the house with his wife. Ben resented the old man suddenly asserting himself, imposing his will, asking shyly for Jane to clean and scrub and cook for this animal from the plains. He hated Silas's spending good money to hire old Della to help Jane, *hiring* a Negro he'd set free.

"She's coming home," Silas said to Ben. "I want it to be like she remembers, like her ma and grandma made it. Clean. Pretty. Smelling good with bread baking. That's how a homecoming ought to be, like that."

"She won't know clean or pretty or smelling good either, Pa," Ben said. "She ain't nothing more than a savage. It'll all be wasted on this woman."

Maybe Ben was right. Sarai had been gone a long time. Maybe she'd forgotten all the little things. But Silas thought that, if he were ever separated from his people, it would be the little things he'd remember. Three quarters of a century after his own childhood, he remembered how his own ma set spring flowers on the table and heated salt bags to put against his feet on the cold nights.

But there was more. Silas knew Ben remembered when the boys came home. It was almost the same then, only Silas rode by himself to Fort Cobb to get them from Zach Taylor. Logan and Kane brought them in, had traded with the Comanches for them. After ten years with the Comanches, Johnny couldn't speak English. He was a wild creature Silas slowly and painfully reclaimed for his dead son, James. Johnny finally made a home for himself, ranching a long way out from Ben and civilization.

The other boy, Ben's son, Jamie ran away before Silas could get him home. Silas dropped his head. Maybe Ben blamed him for letting the boy get off. But he could not stop him, not without tying him hand and foot as Logan and Kane had done.

Dear God, savage — that was the right word for the boy, Jamie. Smooth soft apricot skin, hair lighter than moonlight, eyes blue as Tennessee streams, but he was savage. Not savage as it meant untamed, but more cruel and sinister, hungry for pain and suffering and death. Jamie Stone was a white savage — a man the frontier knew to be far more deadly than any mere Indian. How could Silas tell Ben that?

Once in Tennessee, a mink got into the chickens. By himself the furry beauty killed every hen and left the plump bodies lying, uneaten. He did not kill from hunger or the need to protect himself. He took nothing more than blood from their living throats and the pleasure of killing each one. How could a man tell another man his son was like that animal?

Maybe, Silas thought, he had not tried hard enough to get Jamie home. What was it about the boy that caused him not to tie him and deliver him to Ben. Was it his eyes? Was it the way he had twisted young Johnny's hand under a rope holding the pack saddle to the mule? Maybe his thoughts on the boy's savagery were an excuse for his failure to Ben. Maybe he should have let Ben know the boy, try with him. Maybe Ben would not resent Sarai so if he'd gotten his own boy back. But there it was, Silas thought, the children of the dead brothers sought out and brought home while Ben's son was left with the Comanches. Let go by his own grandfather. That could make a man bitter.

Ben came to hate the Indians after the massacre. He could not reckon it as an impersonal event. Seeing his mother and brothers killed filled him with hate for everything Indian. He hated them for stealing his boy, turning him Indian. He hated Sarai for living with the Comanches. It wasn't rational because she couldn't help it, being a child. But she was an Indian to him for all her white blood. And Ben hated Indians. He hated white people who took up with them even more.

When they came to Texas, back when she still belonged to Mexico, Ben was a fiery young preacher, wanting to spread the word of God among the Papists and heathen. He was the one who led the way to Texas with a mission bigger than family and farm. He drew the others after him in his enthusiasm. They sold out and came along with Ben, the whole family.

Ben alone, among the family left at the Crossing, lived through the April massacre. Silas thought that was a sign of the work God planned for Ben and he told Ben his thoughts. Silas never held it against Ben that he'd led the family to Texas where they were killed. But Ben maybe held it against himself, inside somewhere.

\After the attack, Ben was scared of God. He felt dangerously vulnerable to the whimsy of God and the pain Ben thought he could inflict. He took the killings personally. God had let him down; but God was too powerful to confront. Instead, Ben focused his hate on God's instruments, the Comanches. Sarai, his dead brother's child, was a Comanche.

Ben still preached after the killings, but it was more a way of power in the frontier community than a calling. He preached the word and held to the letter, but he never went far beneath to the meaning. God became Ben's tool, a Giver and a Taker who had to be handled just right.

Ben preached and profited in the eyes of the world, but Silas saw him grow smaller inside with no increase of soul to share, nothing to give anyone. Ben had no more pain, no hurt to bear for others because there were no others. There was only one concern in him, himself — everything, everyone served him, had no worth or value, elicited no emotion, except as it affected him.

Sarai interfered with Ben's plans. On the prairie with

103

the Indians she did not really exist. And if people remembered Sarai, they remembered the massacre, and they felt sorry for Ben and that made them vulnerable to Ben. But coming home she was a problem.

Dealing with Ben was not going to be easy for Silas or Sarai. But, at least, Silas thought, he was here — here one last time to reclaim a lost child. He had lived to see her come home. He would see her brought through for his son John and for himself, if time would hold off a little longer.

Silas saw John again walking across the land with the little white-haired girl child on his shoulders, talking to her, pointing at birds or trees, holding her up to catch a limb, infecting her with the hope of the land and the time. At last waiting became too full of time past, too hard to bear again. Silas could wait no longer. There was today and tomorrow to see to. He rode out to meet the man bringing home the little girl, his granddaughter.

"Sarai-ah. Sarai-ah," he said aloud to himself. "Sarai's home, son. Your baby's come home to us."

Silas Stone reined up near the riders. He stuck out a big paw-like hand and Kane shook it firmly. "Thank you, Kane," Silas said. "You've kept your word, son. Thank you for riding so far when you're tired out."

"You'd have done the same, Silas," said Kane, shifting his weight in the saddle to see what Silas was looking at.

Silas did not hear. He walked his horse closer to the woman. "Sarai-ah," he said softly. The woman's eyes met the old man's.

"Sarai-ah. Oh, child, you look so much like your ma and your grandma, too. Like I knew you would."

"Are you sure it's her, Silas?" asked Kane.

"It's her, son," Silas said. "The same serious little face I used to see over the picture book."

Silas reached into his coat and held out a worn little book toward Sarai. She did not look. The old man wrapped his reins around the saddle horn. Sarai's horse kicked at something at its heel, jostling her and the baby, making her look down at the ragged pages held open in Silas's outstretched hands. Kane watched silently.

Sarai sat the horse, staring at the page of Bible characters, fighting some ancient battle. She sat. Then, she reached out and took the book in her hands. She closed it, ran her hand over the scarred cover, and put the book into the blanket at her waist. She held her hand over the book.

When she looked at Silas again, tears ran down her cheeks.

Sarai Stone said, "Grandfather."

Kane untied the lead rope from his saddle and dropped the line over her pony's neck.

"I'll ride on ahead," he said gruffly.

Chapter Fifteen

Sarai Stone rode beside Silas into the town called Stone's Crossing. Kane still rode ahead. Silas guided her through the little settlement where curious folks stood beside their wagons or doors to catch sight of the lost child.

"Twenty-five years since she rode out of here," a man said to his own child. "Long time 'fore we come. She don't look so bad for the ordeal, does she?" he asked his wife.

"She's carrying a baby on her saddle," his wife said in a hushed voice, and turned away. "Come on, Sam. Silas is a good man. We'll not look on his shame."

Sam lingered.

"He don't seem ashamed. Seems happy. By golly, he seems plum happy."

"Sam," the woman's voice was harsher. "That's an Indian baby. She had that baby by a red Indian."

"It looks like a fine baby. Fat. I reckon she's bound to have formed an affection in twenty-five years," Sam said.

"*An* affection," his wife said, and shrugged knowingly. "Sam, I reckon you're a fool . . . that's some savage's lust proved out." She walked off then, protecting her child from further seeing.

"Still I don't see what choice she had. People being people and all," said Sam, mounting onto the wagon seat.

"Wouldn't expect you to see. But other folks will," said the woman as they drove away from town. "What would you think if *I* had an Indian baby?"

Sam thought about that as he drove on. Finally, he said, "You know any Indians, Judith?"

"We took down the old stockade a few years back," Silas explained to Sarai as they rode among the silent citizens. "Wasn't needed any more. Didn't do any good anyway. Just a grim reminder. Just a tombstone for the family. No need for it for a long, long time. Comanches don't come this way much any more."

Silas looked at the faces as he talked. He saw on many the same judgmental look Ben wore. Ben's congregation, he thought.

"Silas," a voice yelled out from the porch at the general store.

Silas pulled back on his reins, swung his boots forward in the stirrups. The storekeeper dropped the flour sack from his shoulder into the wagon and stepped into the bed to shake Silas's hand.

"By the grace of God, Silas, you got her back after all these years," he said, hitting Silas on the shoulder with his other hand. He nodded toward Sarai, "Miss Sarai."

A little barrier broke down with the storekeeper's words. People came up to Silas's and Sarai's horses, eddying around them, shaking hands and nodding at Sarai. Sarai felt something touching her foot. She looked down. A little girl with moonlight hair was running her fingers over the beaded moccasin with its trailing fringe. She smiled up at the woman. Sarai smiled back.

"You sure it's her?" asked the storekeeper.

"It's her," Silas said, holding the hand Sarai had pushed into his. "She's my lost grandchild, come home."

Sarai looked up at the figure under the shade of the

store porch. Kane, having dismounted his horse, watched her closely. When their eyes met, she looked away up the street. There another man with hands crammed into his pockets leaned against a door jamb. A bright white shirt poked out of the collar and arms of a black wool suit. Sarai had not seen him in twenty-five years, but she remembered Ben Stone.

"Kane," Silas Stone said, "we'll meet you down at the office."

As Kane made his way along the board sidewalk, Silas began to move the horses through the people.

"Thank you, folks," he said. "Thank you. Thank you for your kind wishes."

Kane read the sign from across the street, big gold letters across the window panes: Silas and Ben Stone, Cotton and Land Brokers. Ben went back inside before Silas and Sarai tied up in front. Kane crossed the street and waited for them. They went in together.

The inside of the office was heated by a big stove set in the center of the floor. Its flue pipe shot up into the high ceiling past the small gallery that bent around three sides of the interior. Two clerks stood with their backs to the scene below, working at high desks. Behind the stove, big doors closed over a dock for cotton sellers and their goods. A warehouse out back still held a portion of last fall's crop. The front of the building where Ben sat held two desks and massive leather chairs for Ben and Silas on opposite sides and several smaller but comfortable-looking chairs for their patrons.

The new arrivals naturally went to the desk where Ben sat back, feet propped up on the desk, hands behind his head. He observed them critically as they entered.

"Get up, son," Silas said gently. "Shake hands with

Hugh Kane. He's come a long way to bring home our Sarai."

Ben leaned forward, without dropping his feet or rising, and shook Kane's hand. Kane barely felt the quick hand clasp. Ben didn't smile or nod or speak. Kane's eyes traveled to the big-bore repeater leaning against the corner behind Ben.

"There's a reward, Kane," Silas said, sitting comfortably, taking Sarai's hand. "Been waiting for a long time."

"Silas, you paid me in advance," Kane said. "Remember, your San Jacinto money for my schooling? That's more than enough."

"But you've been searching for such a long time, Kane," Silas said. "I'd like to do more."

"Remember me in your prayers," Kane said. "That'll be enough."

"He's the one who'll need prayers," Ben said dryly. "Pray for him if you know how."

"I know how," Kane said. "Men pray differently, but most of them pray."

"Each man given up to his own ways," said Ben.

"Where's Logan?" asked Silas, before Ben and Kane could square off more directly.

"I don't know," Kane said. "He was supposed to catch up to me before I got here. He went back to line out the surveying crew and get the field notes to file with the land office."

"I'm sure he's fine," Silas said, catching the hint of worry in Kane's words. "He's stayed alive a long time out here by knowing his way around. Logan's not slack handed."

"No, he's not, as a rule," Kane said. "He's kept me alive plenty of times."

"What's the land like?" asked Ben. "Any good for cotton?

"Not for cotton," said Kane. "Ranch country, rolling hills, good grass, good water out of a limestone heart."

"Humph," said Ben. "Cattle don't make the money cotton does."

"Maybe not," said Kane. "It's a different kind of life, ranching and cotton raising. Takes different kinds of men."

"I remember when surveyors got $3.00 for a 1000 reales, $27.00 for a league of land."

"That's a long time ago," Kane answered.

"I guess you make a living," Ben said.

"I guess," Kane said.

"For the quality of work most surveyors provide, the government overpays," Ben said.

"Our surveys will stand the test," Kane said.

"Sure they will," Ben smiled. "Unless you and your men took Injun fright and couldn't hold the rod and compass straight while you were running. Say, Kane, if you don't want the reward, what do you want?"

Kane looked at the critical face of Ben Stone. "I want to keep a promise I made . . . see the lady home with her people."

Ben looked at Sarai who sat holding the little girl.

"Well, she's no lady, but she's home."

Silas frowned. "Be careful of your words, Ben."

"She doesn't understand a word, Pa, not a word," Ben said.

"I understand," Silas Stone said. "And I won't have the girl made light of by her own family."

The father's and son's eyes met across the desk.

"If it pleases you, Pa. Well, I've work to do while

you folks idle away the day," Ben said and stood up, dismissing them.

Kane stood, too.

"Oh, stay to supper, Kane," Silas said. "You've come a long, hard ride. We'll go up to the house. I'd like to talk some."

"Thanks, Silas," Kane said. "But I want to find out what's happened to Logan."

"You got to eat somewhere. Might as well be with me," Silas said, refusing to let Kane get away.

They sat together in the low gathering room of Silas's house. The walls were uncovered limestone. Heavy beams crossed the ceiling holding up the second floor. Jane Stone set food on the table. Her thin mouth was tight and her hands shook slightly as she put the plate before Sarai. Sarai did not remember her. Silas told her through Kane that Jane was Ben's wife after Rachel died.

"Kane," Silas said, "will you tell her for me about the knife and fork? I had the damnedest time trying to get that over to Johnny. He kept digging in with his hands until Ben refused to eat at the same table with him."

Kane spoke softly in Comanche to Sarai. "Your grandfather wants you to learn to eat properly, like a gentlewoman. Take your napkin from beside your plate and put it across your lap." Kane picked up his large white napkin, unfolded it, and laid it in his lap. "Use it to wipe your face and your hands. Hold the fork in your left hand." He demonstrated. "And the knife in your right. Hold the meat or whatever you want to eat with the fork, cut off that piece with the knife like this."

Sarai watched.

111

"Try it," Kane said.

The woman placed her napkin in her lap, over the child's legs. Reaching around her, she picked up the knife and fork and cut the meat as Kane had shown.

"Use the fork to take the bite to your mouth or the child's. It's considered polite to lay the knife down while you put the food in your mouth. Some folks even change the fork to their right hand, before taking the food to their mouths. Like this. Try it."

Sarai tried it.

"You're quick," Kane said. "Now vegetables. You can spear with the fork, if they're in chunks, or you can use the fork or a spoon sideways like a shovel. Scoop it up, put it in your mouth with your right hand. You can herd up the vegetables and sauces with a small piece of bread on your fork. Don't use your knife for that, and never eat off your knife. Ladies don't do that, Sarai."

Summer fretted as another mouthful of food passed her by.

"If you want to," Kane said, "you can cut up the little girl's meat all at the same time . . . that's fine for children . . . and feed her with the fork in your right hand. Sarai, just don't use your fingers to feed yourself. Use the utensils. The bread is the only thing you can touch with your hands. Good manners will be pleasant for your grandfather and fit your place as his granddaughter. You don't want to shame him or yourself."

Sarai said nothing but looked down at Summer.

"Go on," Kane said. "Just eat. I'll watch you till I know you've got it."

Sarai began to feed the little girl. She cut all the meat and fed her a bite at a time, using the fork. Sometimes

112

the child chased it and took it deeply into her soft mouth. The vegetables were tricky at first for Sarai to catch, but gradually she and the little girl got the hang of eating white.

Kane corrected from time to time: "Other hand. Put the fork in the part you're cutting off." Finally, Kane said, "Wipe your mouth. Don't rub it, just touch it gently, lady-like. Look."

He delicately wiped his mouth. Sarai smiled at the attempted feminine gesture, but she imitated her mentor.

"Well," Ben said, entering the scene where the four adults present were concentrated on Sarai's eating manners, "I see we are breaking in another savage. How about some dog, Miss Sarai?"

Kane didn't look up.

"Comanches don't eat dog," he said. Then he shot a hard look into Ben's eyes. "But if they did, she could eat it, by God, with a knife and fork."

"Grown attached to her, have you, Kane? Long ride *alone* to Stone's Crossing, I guess," Ben said, hanging his hat over his coat.

"I don't like your nasty tone," Kane said. "I did not take advantage of this woman."

"Maybe she took advantage of you." Ben winked. "I expect we will have a lot of dogs barking around here from now on. They can smell a bitch in heat a mile off."

"Good God in heaven, Ben," Silas said.

Kane stood up.

"Push further, Stone, and I'll forget this is a good man's house, and you're his son. That kind of talk is for saloons."

"Exactly," said Ben, "and when you've told of the pleasures of your ride with this woman around the tables of the saloons you frequent, that good man and his son will be a laughing stock."

Sarai and Summer watched the scene intently. The child drew back against the woman and carefully, cautiously watched Ben and Kane. Kane laid his napkin on the table and looked at Sarai. He spoke directly to her in Comanche.

"He says you're a bitch dog in heat. And I've had you on the ride in. And that other men will come to have you. And you'll bring shame on him and your grandfather with your promiscuity. That's what your uncle thinks of you, Indian women in general, and Comanche women in particular. That will be a common opinion among people like him because it's an acceptable custom among Indians to share their women. White men don't share anything they value. They think you have no value.

"Now I've said it. I've told you what white people think about your life with the Comanches . . . just one man after another. Unclean. Passed over the prairie." Kane signed furiously as he talked, punctuating his words.

"That is why you behaved as you did on the journey?" Sarai asked.

"No," Kane said emphatically. "That was something else altogether." Sarai raised her head slightly, but said nothing more. "But that's what they think. Some of them are willing to forget it. Some are not. But they all think it. There will be men who'll try you and women who will step to the other side of the ribbon rolls when you come up. How you handle it for yourself and the baby and Silas is up to you." Kane looked down. "Now you know. You are not mine to advise," he said. "But if you were my wife or daughter, I'd tell you what

114

the Mexicans say . . . the best revenge is a life well lived."

"What did you say to her?" Silas asked.

"I told her what Ben and people like him are saying," Kane said. "I told her so she'll know the shame they're putting on her. At least, now she knows what white men think. She's an honorable woman among The People. But you can make her ashamed, Ben Stone, if you try hard enough. I hope to hell, she makes a contest of it and spits in your damned snake eyes."

Chapter Sixteen

Silas Stone led his granddaughter up the wide stairs to the little room she and Summer would share. Kane followed. It was a cozy room with a small fireplace off the main chimney. Silas lit the fire he had built that morning. Sarai stood looking about the room.

Its outer walls were uncovered stone like the lower floor. The inside wall with the door was papered with a small flowered calico print. A ceiling had been boxed in roughly on top of exposed beams. An iron bedstead covered with a bright quilt sat against one wall. Nightgowns for woman and child were carefully laid out. Slippers sat beside the bed. There was a washstand with basin and towels near the door. A wardrobe held down one corner opposite the bed, a rocking chair and small table the other. Beside the fireplace sat a copper bucket filled with wood and next to it a child's chair.

"Kane, tell her the room is hers. The clothes on the bed and in the wardrobe are for her and the child. Everything she'll need for a while is in here. She can come and go as she pleases, but I hope she'll stay, try things out. Explain things, please," Silas said sitting in the rocker. "I'm afraid I'm beginning to feel my age. Tired from the excitement, I expect."

Kane went to the wardrobe and opened it. "These clothes are yours and the child's," he said in Comanche. He pulled out the bottom drawer. "These are to wear under the clothes. They are called underwear . . . drawers, camisole, petticoat, stockings for your legs. Here are shoes. How the hell did he know what size you'd be?

"Oh," Kane said, drawing forth the chamber pot from the corner beside the wardrobe, "this is for elimination. You go in this in the night if you have to. Next morning you carry it out and empty it at the backhouse. Generally, you can find a backhouse by the smell."

Kane crossed to the bed, lifted one corner of the long sleeved white nightgown with pink lace ribbons.

"You both wear these to sleep in. White people wear night clothes. These are night clothes. When you go to bed, you turn back the top covers and crawl between." Kane pushed the mattress. "This is a feather bed," he said. "It's kind of like being swallowed alive, but its soft and warm."

At the wash basin, Kane lifted the pitcher and poured water into the bowl. "This is for washing. This is soap. And these towels are for scrubbing or drying off.

"Anything else I should show her, Silas? I really need to be heading on out," Kane said.

"Just tell her, I want her to be comfortable here," Silas said, looking at Sarai. "Ben will get over being mad. He's your blood. He can't change that. Blood will out in the end."

Kane echoed Silas's words in Comanche.

Silas rose from the chair and walked with Kane toward the door. Silas had his arm around Kane's shoulders.

"This has meant everything to me," he said.

At the door Silas paused.

"One more thing, son," he said. "Before you go, tell her I love her and the child. And I thank God I've lived to see her home."

Kane turned to Sarai who stood by the bed and spoke Silas's words. Then the men went away.

Sarai went to the window, pushed back the curtains that hid the twilit prairie. Setting Summer on the floor, she tried to open the window, but found two heavy nails held it prisoner. For a long moment her misty eyes ran over the distant fading sky to the west. She saw Kane ride away.

Sarai turned back at last to the room. Before her lay all the years she had missed, and all the things she must learn again, to live white. It seemed too much that winter night. Sarai closed her eyes.

Summer pulled at her hand. Sarai looked down. The child led her to the small chair beside the fire. She squatted over her little feet with her hands across her lap and studied the chair closely. She did not touch it or try to sit in it. Sarai smiled and kneeled on the braided rug beside the child. She ran her hands over the back and down the arm of the chair Silas had made for her, caressing the old friend.

"Sit," Sarai said, and lifted the child into her old chair.

The little girl giggled and wrapped her fat fingers around the arms of the chair. Sarai touched her knee. "Wait." She pulled the little book from her waist. She arranged herself beside the child and opened the book.

"Book," she said. "Good."

Summer looked intently at the pages as Sarai turned them. Sometimes Sarai spoke in Comanche, explaining the nearly forgotten, once familiar drawings to her child.

Silas knocked on the door. He opened it slowly.

"Just came to say good night, my dears," he said. "See you in the morning."

Sarai nodded and smiled softly. Silas closed the door. It irritated her that she could not get Silas's words. She felt that Silas meant well. But she wanted the words. She wanted to understand. Kane's voice spoke to her,

"Your grandfather says that he loves you and the child. He thanks God he has lived to see you come home."

She heard more words beyond the door and went to listen. Searching for any word she knew, Sarai listened.

" 'Night," Silas said.

She heard him walk toward the stairs and stop. Someone else was close to the door.

"Don't lock her in, Ben. She's had too many locks and chains the last few days. This is her home. She must be free to come and go just like the rest of us. If you're scared, lock your own door."

The one outside, Ben, went away. Sarai heard Silas descend the stairs. Across the hall, a lock bolt clicked softly in the door to Ben's and Jane's bedroom. Sarai turned back to the room. Summer's head had fallen forward in sleep. The little book rested in her lap.

Sarai lifted the sleeping child from the chair and carried her to the bed. She removed the child's clothes and dressed her in the smaller nightgown and placed her beneath the covers. Slowly Sarai removed her own clothes and put on her night gown. She caught a glimpse of herself in the mirror as the gown fell over her body. Sarai went to the mirror. She touched her face. Picking up the hair brush, she brushed her light hair a few sharp strokes, pulled the cropped hair behind her ears with one hand.

Where was the Niminah woman in these clothes, in this room? She looked more closely. The red paint on her cheeks and on the part of her hair had washed away days before. The eyebrows plucked clean as a woman of The People, the walnut stained tattoo along her eye lashes to imitate the dark lashes of The People remained. Sarai pulled open the throat of the night dress. Her skin was white. She ran her fingers over it. The big gold ring on the first finger of her hand caught the light. Nobah had given it to her. She turned the ring, moved it on her finger. It was easily removed. She held it in her palm. Could nothing permanent, no outward sign, mark the years among The People? Could she seem so white merely by putting on different clothes?

Sarai replaced the ring and walked to the bed where Summer slept. The child was beautiful, dark hair pouring out on the white pillow. Sarai smiled, stroked the hair from the forehead. Her children were real, she thought. She had not dreamed. The children were real. The years were real.

The People were real, too. Somewhere across the dark night they existed; they were. They ate and laughed and told stories and slept together, warm and contented. She felt Nobah's arms around her. Her mind played the old scenes for her. And then she remembered — fearful retreats, hunger, Pia dead, Soldier's Coat dead, Nobah slumped, riding before the men in battle, dead children scattered like buckskin dolls on the ground.

Sarai wanted to hold Summer close. She lay down beside her. The great bed rose up around them. Sarai got up, lifted the sleeping child and drew the buffalo robe from the end of the bed. She lay down by the fire. Crying softly, she fell asleep.

Logan shivered, tied hand and foot beside the tattered teepee.

"Hell's bells," he muttered. "Nobah, get your butt out here and untie me before I freeze to death. You damned savage, untie me or kill me. By God, it's again' a man's dignity to be trussed up like a turkey or something. I wouldn't do this to you or a dog for that matter. Hell, my dog always came in by the fire."

The door flap lifted and Sees-the-Enemy caught the rope around Logan's neck.

"Jerk the shit out of it," Logan said to himself. "I'm raw meat already, you bastard."

Sees-the-Enemy cut the leather thong and lifted Logan through the door, dropped him inside.

"Well, thank you, you bastard," said Logan. "You're a Christian gentleman."

Sees-the-Enemy caught Logan by the head, dragged him away from the door, and threw him against the wall of the lodge.

Across the fire Logan saw Nobah. Leaning back against a willow rest, he had a buffalo robe drawn up over his right shoulder. His left arm and shoulder were naked, the arm resting across the robe. Sweat sparkled over his face and the bare arm.

Sees-the-Enemy kneeled by the fire and scooped a broth from a simmering pot. He wiped off the ladle and carried it to Nobah. He lifted it to Nobah's lips.

"What's the matter, chief?" asked Logan, suddenly alert. "You added a new ceremony of service?"

"Shut up, Logan," Sees-the-Enemy said. "You are a barking dog. Sometimes barking dogs get their tongues cut out."

The lodge flap opened again and another warrior came in. He held prickly pear pads on an arrow. He squatted and held them over the fire to burn away the thorns.

"Hot damn," Logan said. "You're making a poultice. Hot damn, Nobah, you've got a wound. So that's why you didn't go after the woman yourself, but settled for me. Ha!"

Sees-the-Enemy kicked Logan in the chest.

"Quiet."

Logan coughed. "I'm quiet as a mouse. That's right."

Sees-the-Enemy threw a robe over Logan's head, hiding the treatment of Nobah from him.

"Shoot. It's my damned feet that are cold, you bloody bastard. Besides I know something of doctoring. I've seen enough of it around Kane."

Chapter Seventeen

During the night snow began to drift down across the farmstead. By morning the ground was covered with several inches of whiteness, and it continued to snow. The sky remained almost black, and wind whipped down from the north. Ben sat on the side of the bed. The candle cast flickering shadows over the rough walls.

"I'll see to the stock," Ben said to Jane. "You have a good hot breakfast ready when I come in."

Jane, already dressed, stood at the door. "How many years we been married, Ben?" she asked.

Ben looked up at the bony woman, almost grotesque in the eerie light. "Most of our lives, I guess," he said, and thought about the question. "Near about twenty-four years."

"Near about," Jane said, turning the key in the lock. "And every morning all those years you've seen to the stock, and I've made you and Silas a good hot breakfast. You think I might do it out of habit without bein' told just once?"

"What's got into you?" Ben asked, mildly irritated.

"Old age most likely," Jane said. "I just feel old and somehow lost out this morning. Reckon it will pass after I eat my nice hot breakfast."

Jane left Ben and went downstairs.

"Old woman's getting crazy like Pa," Ben said to himself. "Whole bunch of things getting crazy like Pa. Ben, you are going to have to take a hand."

Ben found his father asleep in the rocking chair when

123

he went into his room.

"Wake up, Pa. We got us a good storm blowin' in."

Silas opened his eyes.

"I'm awake," he said. "Smelled Janey's coffee on the fire. Need any help at the barn?"

"No," Ben said. "I can handle it by myself. You got that Indian to see to."

Silas rubbed his eyes slowly with the finger tips of one hand.

"She's your blood, Ben. Your dead brother's only child. Your niece. She needs us, and we need her."

"Can't see how, after twenty-five years," said Ben sullenly.

He left his father and went to the barn. He leaned hard against the wind and snow as Jane watched him from the window. She saw him stop once and look back at the house, then he ducked his head and went on.

"Jane," Silas shouted from the stairs. "Jane, Sarai's gone with the child. Get Ben. We've got to find her. She can't make it without shelter in this storm."

Silas was almost frantic at this second loss of his granddaughter, at her prospects in the snow storm.

Jane grabbed her shawl from the chair back and threw it over her head. She ran and stumbled across the snow in Ben's deep tracks and burst into the barn. Ben had just begun the milking. The old cow's breath frosted in the still air. Ben held his hand to the Guernsey's warm flank.

"She's gone! Sarai's gone!" Jane said.

"And good riddance," Ben said, turning to his chore. "I thought I saw a track in the snow."

"Get up, Ben. Your father needs your help," Jane said, almost pleading.

124

"Cow needs milkin'," he said, looking at the animal. Jane waited, saying no more. At last finished, Ben picked up his pail and stool and sat them against the wall. "Let's go help Pa, then," he said, and they went back into the storm.

Ben and Jane met Silas coming from the house. The three stood with the storm swirling about them. Ben pointed toward the river and yelled above the wind.

"I think I saw a track going off that way."

"Let's go on out," said Silas.

He and Ben waded across the deepening snow toward the trees that marked the line of water wandering through the land.

"See anything?" Silas shouted after a while.

"Maybe we'll see some tracks under the trees," Ben said.

The sheltering grove blocked the wind and the snow's direct blast. The men relaxed a little and began to look around.

"What's that?" Ben asked.

Silas looked in the direction Ben faced. He stepped up even with his son, squinting out the light shapes against the dark water.

"Do you see? Down there." Ben pointed. "I think it's moving. Maybe she fell in the water, Pa."

Ben and Silas moved quickly toward the downstream object. Silas stooped to pick up a limb lying nearly covered by the snow. Ben went on rapidly, sliding off the upper bank onto another that paralleled the stream. Silas stripped away the small branches from the main limb as he followed Ben.

By the time he caught up, Ben stood rigidly still.

"Daughter of perdition," he said and turned toward his father.

Silas looked beyond Ben. Sarai and her child were in the icy water, bathing. The buffalo robe and their clothing lay in the shelter of the bushes. Sarai washed the child oblivious to the storm, the men, or her own nakedness.

"Daughter of sin. Child of iniquity," said Ben as he strove up the bank and headed back toward the farm.

Silas looked at Ben, then back toward Sarai and the child, faint shapes in the falling snow.

"Sarai," he shouted above the storm.

The larger shape lowered itself in the water, pulling the child after her. Silas bent toward the clothes and buffalo robe. He picked up the garments and laid them nearer the water's edge.

"Get dressed," he said, turning his back and walking away up the bank. "I'll wait up here for you."

In a short while Sarai joined her grandfather, and they walked silently back through the storm to the house. Inside the kitchen, a steaming coffee mug sat where Ben had been. Jane did not look up from her work. Silas removed Sarai's robe and hung it up. He hung his coat and hat beside it.

"Sit down, Sarai," he said.

"Not at this table," Ben shouted from behind them. "Not at a decent Christian table."

"Comanches are clean people, Ben. She's used to bathing in the open in all kinds of weather. She meant no immodesty," Silas said.

Ben threw the large tin bath basin on the table, knocking over the coffee cup. Jane grabbed it and began wiping up the spilled coffee, muttering to herself.

"This was under the bed all the time," he shouted. "If she's so clean, why didn't she use this? It was there for her."

126

Silas touched the rim of the basin. "I expect that we didn't tell her, and she didn't know to look under the bed," he said.

"I don't want her here," Ben said. "What if some man had come along and seen her like that? You know what would have happened. Then what? Would you expect me to stand up for her? How could I do that, knowing what she's done, what she's been? Don't you know the bucks looked on her like that, naked? She ain't one of us. She's an Indian, a godless heathen Indian. She's got to be broke of it . . . saved from the sin of her ways before she can live in this house or sit at this table."

"As long as I live," said Silas softly, "Sarai Stone and her child will be welcome in this house and at this table. Her daddy and mother gave their lives for this home. She's a right here."

"She's given her body to savages in lust. The child's the proof of her sin," Ben said. "My God, Pa, they share their women among their brothers, even friends. Pa, remember what they did to Ma . . . staked her to the ground with a lance and took turns at her, her an old woman. That's what this *thing* comes from. That's how she's lived."

The violence of Ben's words and actions made Sarai start to shake inside more than the icy water and wind. There was something more in his voice now, more than anger. There was hate and condemnation. It had the scent of shame and dishonor about it. The same as that given by the Comanches to a woman who deceived her husband or to a warrior who betrayed his trust.

Kane's words whispered through Sara's mind: " 'He says you're a bitch dog in heat. And I've had you on the ride in. And that other men will come to have you.

127

And you'll bring shame on him and your grandfather with your promiscuity. That's what he thinks of you, Indian women in general, and Comanche women in particular.' "

"Let off, Ben," said Silas, sitting down. "Even your own Bible doesn't condemn a woman for something she can't help. It says so plain about slave women. And the old Hebrews held to the custom of Leverite, a man taking his dead brother's wife as his own."

"Pa, you don't remember because you weren't here. You didn't see Ma after they finished. She was buried before you even came home. All of them were. You can forgive because you didn't see. Now you've brought it all back. I can't forget it. I can't forgive it, not without something more than pity for this thing," Ben said. "Without repentance, there's no forgiveness of sins. When you take her side, you're just an instrument of the devil, tempting me to go soft on sin."

"She doesn't know she needs to repent," Silas said. "But right now she's open to learn our ways. You can win her with love and patience, Ben. Put aside all this guilt and fear and shouting."

"I can't handle it, Pa. I can't handle the shame and trouble she's going to bring. I've lived a moral life, set an example. I can't handle the shame of what's coming with her, sure as anything. It ain't right to ask me."

Ben took his hat and coat and left the kitchen.

Silas looked at Sarai, at Jane.

"You hold with that?" he asked Jane who stood with her back to him washing the few breakfast dishes.

"Ben's my husband. His is the thinkin', Silas. Mine is the obeying," she said.

Silas looked down at the floor. The lines were drawn. To save Sarai, he must further destroy what relation there was with his only son.

"I'm going into Murphytown in the morning," he said to Jane. "You want anything special, you make a list, and I'll pick it up."

Silas took Sarai's arm.

"Murphytown? That's a long way in a bad storm like this. You best wait," Jane said, turning toward Silas.

"At my age, I don't have time to wait," said Silas. "This time of year a storm can blow over and the flowers be up by tomorrow. When I get back, we're going to have to make some changes. You and Ben think about that. I suppose the old place across the river will suit Sarai and me best for a while."

"Oh, Silas, you always want to get back to the old place like it was the best thing in the whole world. There's nothing over there but a couple of shacks and two old black people. You know Ben hates it 'cause you let old Jack race horses over there," said Jane, dismissing Silas's plan.

"When Jo Martin ran up on that Comanche village, he put Sarai on a different path. I got to help her walk it," Silas said, almost to himself. "At her age, a full grown adult woman, she's got to learn things a child knows, and her pride will fight that, rebel against having to start over. That's hard enough. But this shame. This guilt Ben puts on her is deadly. I wish you could help me, Jane."

Jane made a small, snorting sound.

"Heavens, Silas, I don't know what you're talking about. Besides, Ben won't have it. And he's my husband. I'm obliged to obey Ben. Book says it . . . 'wives obey your husbands.' " Jane shut her thin mouth tightly and scrub-dried a wooden bowl. "Book says it."

"I reckon that keeps you from having to take any

responsibility for your own deeds, Jane. Just find some rule and hold tight whatever comes. I hope Ben can stand the weight of both your souls come the Judgment."

Silas led Sarai from the kitchen.

"Piffle!" said Jane to herself, setting a plate in the plate rack. "Book says it. Wives be obedient to your husbands."

Chapter Eighteen

Sarai rocked all day, looking out the little bedroom window. At first light, she saw Silas leave. All day she watched for him. At noon, Jane brought a tray, set it by the door, knocked, and fled. Sarai and Summer ate, practicing the words and actions Kane had left them. The sun went down, casting a lingering twilight over the snow. But Silas did not come home. In darkness, illuminated only by the firelight, Sarai could not see outside beyond the window shaped light drawn on the snow, but still she sat beside the window, waiting for Silas.

Men's voices and shuffling noises downstairs caused her to turn away from the window. She stood and went to the door, leaving Summer playing before the fire. Sarai moved silently into the hall and to the landing. The front door stood open with snow and wind whipping into the house.

"Farmer found him about a mile out," said the storekeeper, Elbert Tell, holding a lantern high for the men beyond Sarai's view.

"Looked like his horse fell or threw him," said one of the men with him. "He must have hit his head, broke his neck on something in the snow."

Ben stood in his shirt sleeves and suspenders with his supper napkin tucked over his chest. One hand rested on the heavy wooden plank door. Sarai kneeled to see the men on the porch, staggering under Silas's weight. A companion's lantern bobbed against the wind and blackness.

"Don't believe he suffered a bit. He had a good death. Out doing till the last, that was Silas's way," Tell said.

The husky farmers brought Silas's body into the house. Sarai strained to see the man, but they carried him quickly past, leaving wet chunks of dirty snow melting in the hallway.

"Lay the body on the table," said Ben. "Clear a way there, Jane."

Sarai started silently down the stairs. All the men had their hats off and stood respectfully beyond Silas as Ben bent over the table.

"I hope I go just as easy," said one of the farmers. "Silas was never diminished."

"How come he was out so late in this weather, Ben?" asked the storekeeper.

Ben looked up from his father's still body. Anger flashed through his cold eyes. He jerked the napkin from his shirt and threw it on the floor.

"Harlot. Harlot," he said, knocking over a chair and stumbling toward the hall.

Sarai saw him coming and darted instinctively toward the stairs. Ben took the stairs two at a time behind her. He reached out and tripped her hard against the bare edges of the treads. Then he had her, and pushed her past him down the stairs.

"Get out, you murderess. You killed him. You did it," Ben shouted, shoving Sarai before him. He opened the front door and threw her out. "Out! Get out!"

Ben slammed the door and dropped the bar across it. Sarai lay in the snow where she fell. Then with all her force, she hit the door. She pounded on it, shouting above the wind.

The men inside looked at each other and at Ben who walked quietly into the room and kneeled beside Silas's body. Great tears ran along the creases in Ben's face.

"Bring me that damned papoose, Jane," he said with deadly quiet. "I want everything that smells of Indian out of this house."

Jane scurried past the heavily bundled storekeeper and farmers up the stairs. She caught up Summer and the Indian clothes that hung in the wardrobe and returned nearly breathless to Ben. She stood silently, and waited.

"By their fruits shall ye know them," Ben said. "She's brought death, the black fruit of death, to this house. We know her now for the devil she is. 'Give no place to the devil,' " Ben added for those present, "though your own heart cries out pity. Give her the child, Jane."

As the woman walked silently to the door Sarai's child caught at her straggling hair with fat baby fingers. In the hall, Jane turned and looked back toward Ben who bowed his head over his hands. She looked at the baby. She started to speak, but stopped and turned back to the door.

"Good God, Ben," said the farmer. "It's a norther blowin' out there. You can't shut nobody out tonight."

Ben kept at his prayers, leaving the farmer to look at the others for support. Jane put her hand on the door bar and stood there, thinking. Sarai still beat on the other side.

"You ought to do your own dirty work, Ben," Jane said to herself. "You ought to do it yourself, shut out a nice, gentle child in a storm."

"Just a minute there, Mrs. Stone," the storekeeper said. "I can't believe this can happen. That's a woman and a little child you're putting out in the cold. There's no reason to it."

"Hold fast," Ben admonished himself. "Hold fast, Ben Stone, when you're tempted."

133

He stood up and spoke with burning eyes to the three men.

"You do not know what spirit you are of. Get thee behind me, Satan. It is not I who condemns her, but her life, her deeds."

"They'll freeze to death," the storekeeper said simply.

"So be it," Ben said. "Thy will be done, Lord. It is meet and just to do thy will."

"Damn it, Ben, it ain't God's will," said one of the farmers. "It's yours."

"You ain't been in church enough to recognize God's will, Charlie Legg," Ben said.

"And by God you're the reason," said Legg. "Your brand of religion sours my stomach."

"Easy, Charlie," the storekeeper said. "Bad words won't solve our problem, and they'll be remembered hard come daylight."

"Give me that child," Charlie said, taking Jane's arm. "I'll see they don't freeze to death. I'll take 'em to my place."

"She'll murder you in your sleep," said Ben, advancing toward the men who moved into the hall. "Think of your wife and children. See 'em lying in their own blood."

Legg hesitated. "Me and my oldest boy'll take turns watchin' her."

"Can you be sure, Charlie? She has all the cunning of a Comanche. She nearly got the best of the Rangers with a knife. Rangers, Charlie. Twenty-five years among the Comanches, Charlie. Twenty-five years of killin' her own people, slippin' in with just a bare knife and killin' a whole family, jubilatin' in warm human blood, white people's blood. Can you chance it, Charlie?" asked Ben.

Charlie Legg released Jane's arm. "We can't leave

her out there," he said weakly. "But I got my own to think of first."

"I've got shackles at my store. We can chain her up in my shed where we kept Elkhart's runaway," said Elbert Tell.

"Go, then, out of this house," Ben said. "Mind I warned you what will come. You've sealed your fate."

The storekeeper opened the barred door and pulled Sarai inside by one wrist. "Get some rope out of your wagon, Charlie," he said, holding Sarai's arm behind her, jerking it as she reached for the child.

When the man returned, they tied Sarai's hands with a short rope and gave her the baby. Summer clung to her mother's neck, and Sarai clutched her against herself with the bound hands. One of the men wrapped the blanket and buffalo robe over Sarai's shoulders. They dragged her to the wagon and lifted her onto the bed.

"Aiy, God, the wagon's all mired up," said Legg.

"That Ben's a hard man," said the other farmer. "He never even thanked us for bringin' in his pa's body. Nor offered so much as a hot cup of coffee for our chill."

Neither of the others spoke. They tucked their heads deeper into their coat collars, studying the wagon.

"We ain't goin' to make it in this wagon," said Legg. "I'm goin' to unhitch and ride on home before the weather gets any worse."

"Can you make it back to your store, Elbert, if I take a horse and head on out to my place?" asked the other man. "No use me goin' back toward town, if you can. Just double my time."

"I wouldn't want to put you out, Glen," said the storekeeper bitterly. "Go on and good riddance to you both."

135

The two farmers began to unhitch the big Percherons. The storekeeper pulled Sarai from the wagon and pushed her ahead of him toward the lights of the little town. The mile to his store took almost an hour of hard, stumbling struggle. Elbert Tell unlocked his weathered-board shed with numb fingers and shoved Sarai and the child inside. He followed, pushing her toward a thick post set deep in the ground. Holding his lantern aloft, he found the stiffly frozen chain fastened through an iron ring driven securely into the wood. He snapped the shackle quickly around Sarai's ankle. She struck at him with her free leg. He easily moved beyond her reach.

"I suppose old Ben was right about you," the storekeeper said. "You *are* dangerous."

Sarai jerked at the chain.

"*Won't do you no good, Miss Sarai Stone.* Elkhart's nigger was close to six feet five and two hundred and eighty pounds, and it held him. I'd give you fire, but likely you'd burn the place down."

He walked to a stack of hay piled against the wall and started throwing it toward the woman.

"You're used to living out. I reckon with the hay and that robe you can make it."

The storekeeper raised the lantern.

"Somewheres out here my clerk put some stinkin' old buffalo hides. You're in luck tonight, sister," he said, as he spotted the pile of hides and took three of the stiff, dusty skins and dropped them within Sarai's reach. "That'll keep you."

Tell stepped out and locked the door behind him.

Holding Summer close to her, Sarai sank to her knees in the dirt. The moan of an animal caught in a trap came from the woman as she slowly fell forward onto her hands and touched her head to the floor. The faint sound, almost like *"please,"* sent a shudder through the storekeeper as he made his way back to the store and the promise of snug warm rooms upstairs.

Sarai lay silently. Finally she began to rake the straw together. She found the buffalo skins and piled them on the straw. Sarai tucked Summer inside and crawled beneath to wait for Death, or morning.

Chapter Nineteen

The boy, Joe Ramsey, sat down. He looked at the buzzards and crows that had gathered around the burned surveyors' wagons. The bodies of the surveyors were covered with the black birds, scavenging the windfall Nobah had left them on the prairie. Joe scrubbed his eyes with his freckled hands. He'd walked for three days after the attack and this was where he'd gotten — right back where he started. He lowered his head and let the tears run out unchecked. Three days hard walking, sleeping in the brush like a dog. Three days with nothing to eat but a stinking handful of prairie potatoes. Three days.

The grinding grip of his stomach took his mind off the futile march. Maybe it was lucky he'd come back. Maybe there was food left in the wagon. Something. Anything. Joe Ramsey got up and walked toward the camp. He jerked the burned box where the cook had kept his things. The door came off. Ramsey let it fall as he searched the box. The sugar sack was scorched, the sugar crystallized, but he tasted the chunk anyway. It was good.

He licked the block as he rummaged the charred contents of the wagon. Everything was burned on top. The cook's body hung out of the wagon by one heel. It was burned, too. A long gash had opened the body cavity and the viscera had fallen out and been chewed and eaten by scavengers.

Joe Ramsey didn't look at the body as he lifted charred

sacks and boxes, trying to find something unburned beneath. At last, he uncovered a bag, a big bag of jerked beef. He ripped a chunk from a strip and soaked it in his jaw. The salty, smoked taste soothed him. He rested, relishing the savory taste. There was nothing else. But Joe knew he was lucky. He had found the jerky.

He held the bag tight to him and went to the other wagon. He didn't climb up, but worked over the side. Nothing was left. The supply boxes that held their blankets lay on the ground. They had been pried open and their contents tumbled out and taken by the Comanches. Joe shivered.

He looked about the death camp. Each body had been stripped and split open. After the birds and beasts had had their feast, it was hard to tell just what else had happened after he ran. They were all dead before the Indians let him go. Joe knew that and was thankful for the mercy of quick deaths.

Some of the men's private parts had been cut off, thrown away, or stuffed into their own mouths. Why'd the Comanches do that? Joe wondered. Why wasn't killing a man enough? Something they believed, the boy concluded, like scalping most likely.

He spotted a coat thrown beside one of the men. Joe wanted the coat. Hunching his shoulders against the wind, he went to it, causing the scavengers to part as he walked among them. They did not fly, but simply separated, moved off a few feet, closed again behind him.

Joe lifted the coat. It's contents poured out — a human heart and brain. Joe threw down the coat and gagged and puked the jerky from his empty stomach. Sweat stood on his forehead as he rested over his hands.

At last, Joe got up. Still clutching the jerky, making himself look at the sky and not the ground, he grabbed the coat again by its collar. The boy was not finicky, could not afford to be, not on the frontier, not alone, not in winter. He walked swiftly from the death camp, stumbled down the ravine's edge and started walking away again.

The sky was blue, but the wind was cold. It dried Joe's sweat and left his teeth chattering. He dogged on, holding the jerky, dragging the coat. Hours passed as he walked, occasionally stopping to pound himself, blow his fingers, stamp his feet to life.

Finally he stopped and put the coat on over his own. It was Bill Reynold's coat and Bill was a big man. That was lucky, the boy thought. He tried not to think about the deep stains on the coat.

Joe Ramsey took hold of his mind. He had to get home, get back. He had to make it. He could not keep walking in circles. There was only one thing to do. He had to walk at night, after the stars came out until they set before dawn, keep his bearings by the stars. That was it. He had to keep his bearings by the stars. This time with the stars and the jerky and the coat, he could make it.

The first snow flakes began to fall gently before the wind cut in from the north. Joe felt the wind against his back like a hand almost shoving him toward the settlements to the southeast. He kept walking. He had to walk, he told himself. He had to make time at night while there were stars. And then Joe noticed that he could not see the stars. He stopped. He listened. The wind did not sound like wind any more. It sounded bigger in the blackness. And the blackness became white in front of Joe's eyes. He turned his head; snow swirled on every side. He was in its midst, surrounded by the snow. He had to find cover.

Joe ran. His feet felt solid, lifeless, like the wooden leg the sailor had had in Galveston. It occurred to Joe he might be running in the wrong direction. He could not tell. But he told himself that it did not matter now. He had to have cover. Tomorrow he could set his direction again.

Joe was young. He could run a long time. But his chest hurt from the cold. His legs trembled as he lifted them and shook as he reset them on the earth. It must be that the days without eating had taken more of his strength than he thought.

But Joe was young. He could still run if he could just see a little. Joe fell hard over something already buried in the snow. He rested on his stomach, hearing his heart and breath, letting the pain leave his shins. He felt for the jerky bag against his chest and found it still there.

Joe sat up. If he could see, he thought, he might be near cover right then. He put out his hand and groped the white darkness around him, extending his arms as far as he could.

His hand struck something hard and cold. The boy moved closer. He ran his hand along the object. Slowly it curved under his raw fingers. The boy stopped holding the cold iron curve of the rim. His other hand reached for the spokes. Joe Ramsey dropped his head. Then silently he crawled beneath the burned-out wagon.

With the whirling confusion lifted from his head, he wondered if things would have been different if he had thought of the night walk and stars three days ago. He wondered who would find him, or if he would ever be found. Joe wondered if a man who was never found, lost in the vastness of the prairie, had even existed. How could Joe prove he had ever been, to anyone or even himself, because there was no one and there were no reference points, not even a tombstone, just the howling wind and the blinding snow. Nothing else! Panic rose in Joe's heart.

"Of course, I've been," he said, calming himself. "Not long, but some. God knows Joe Ramsey has been. God knows."

Chapter Twenty

On the second day, the storm stopped in the night and the sun came brightly through the cracks in the storekeeper's shed. The air was warmer. Melting snow already made wet stains along the walls. Sarai's stomach chewed itself in its emptiness as her eyes followed a dusty sun ray from the wall to the ground. Her child had ceased to cry and lay quietly against her. Sarai had been hungry before, but she had never been trapped, chained, and left.

Sarai had seen the Comanches trade captives. Much depended on the owner — some were cruel; some were not. Two women with children were taken with Sarai and John and Jamie Stone in the raid at Stone's Crossing. The raiders raped the women many times. The children saw. The children heard.

The second night out on the plains the smallest child cried too much with hunger. The brave who claimed it and the frantic mother bashed its head against a rock and went to sleep. Sarai remembered. Holding John's hand, she stood and silently watched. The two children saw the still, dead baby and the mother empty of emotions beside it.

The woman grew worse daily as the raiding party drove into the plains. Finally she sat down and would not get up, and the brave split her unresisting head with a tomahawk. And the child Sarai became more silent, watching the strange people, trying not to cry when the hunger hurt, realizing the hard testing for those who would survive.

Now she was once again in an alien world, a prisoner. Her grandfather was dead. Ben had put her out in the storm. The other men had put her here in the shed. What must she do? The answer was simple — survive with the child and escape. There was nothing more for her here. Silas was gone. The promise was finished.

The door to the shed opened and Tell entered. Sarai did not move as the storekeeper set a bowl of mush and a partial loaf of bread beside a bucket of water on the floor within her reach. He stood looking at the heap of skins under which she lay, listening.

"You dead?" he asked. "Hey." He stepped tentatively closer and kicked the skins. "Get up, I brought you some eats." He kicked harder.

Sarai threw the skins back and caught his heel. She jerked with her whole strength, dropping Tell backwards on his bald head. He scrambled quickly away to safety against the wall.

"I don't have to take this," he said. "You ain't none of mine. You're just here because I'm too Christian a man to let you freeze to death. It was an act of mercy. Now, by God, Ben Stone can take care of his own."

The man left the shed and locked the door.

Sarai sat still until he was gone. Then she pulled the cold mush and bread to her. She used the bread for a spoon and slowly fed the child she held. They ate until there was nothing left in the dented, chipped, enameled pan. And they drank from the bucket using the empty pan for a dipper. Sarai washed the child's face and hands and put her gently under the skins to sleep away the time.

A new noise outside occupied Sarai's attention. Men a hundred yards away were digging and cursing. She watched them through the wide gap between the shed's boards. They dug for a long time, taking turns with pick and shovel and jug until the hole was so deep the digger disappeared within it. Finally, the men went away. Sarai crawled in beside Summer and fell asleep.

The sound of singing awakened her — soft, distant singing. Sarai listened. Her forehead drew together as she concentrated on the sound. She suddenly knew the song and sat up. She knew.

> Hope with a gentle persuasion
> whispers her comforting words:
> Wait 'til the darkness is over.
> Wait 'til life's tempest is done.

The words and their meaning came flooding over her as the song drifted across the still air.

> Then when the night is upon us,
> why should the heart sink away?
> When the dark midnight is over,
> watch for the breaking of day.

Sarai said the words softly, slowly. Her grandfather had sung the song often in his deep, full, baritone in church, and while he worked. They had talked about the words of his favorite hymn.

"It means don't quit when things are tough. Get up and go after 'em again. Day will break after the darkest night. God's seen to that."

It was her grandfather's voice she heard again as now she moved to see through the cracks between the boards. Tears gathered in Sarai's blue eyes and rolled down softly over her cheeks. She saw the doors of the white wooden church open, saw the crowd trickle out and follow the pine coffin across the flat prairie toward the grave. She watched from the shed, called the child to her and held her as the singers sang, and the long box disappeared into the ground.

The death song, kept for Elimah and the others escaped for Silas, burst the still air. Mourners around the grave looked up, listening, trying to place the sound. And when they knew, their looks fell to the ground. At the end, they came up and shook hands with Ben and Jane, and went slowly away.

Sarai saw the storekeeper hang back until the others were gone and come to Ben. They talked closely together. He pointed to the shed, growing red in the face. Finally Ben turned away and started for the shed with Tell nearly running beside him still talking. As he strode across the muddy earth, his black coat flared out from his body, like the wings of a bird of prey. Sarai held the child tighter.

> When the night is upon us,
> why should the heart sink away?
> Watch for the breaking of day.

The shed door rattled as Tell unlocked it. And then Ben Stone stood in it, filling the frame, blocking out the sky behind him. Sarai rose and faced him with a face as firm as his own. He waited.

"We got it, Ben," Tell said, handing Ben something — a circle of iron. Ben turned it in his hand, running the cold metal through his palms. He stepped into the room. Tell and a tall young man, wearing a white apron over his clothes, followed. Ben held the iron circle out flat and opened it like a great jaw.

146

Sarai's head went up higher, and she backed away the length of the chain. Tell moved along one side of the shed. The boy along the other. Sarai made no effort to move as they grabbed her already bound arms. She drew herself up straight and tall.

Sarai never took her eyes from Ben Stone as he came toward her with the open ring of iron. He stopped in front of her and slowly raised the ring toward her throat, opening it wider. Sarai lifted her head as he placed its coldness around her neck and clamped it shut. Ben smiled crookedly.

Sarai spat in his face. His hand came up instantly, slapping her backward into the other men's grips. Sarai blinked, but showed no sign of fear. A small trickle of blood ran from the corner of her soft mouth as she smiled back at Ben.

"A collar will not make me an animal, Uncle," said Sarai Stone.

Tell and the boy looked at each other. The words, the thought were full, intelligent, and in English.

"Pride," Ben said. "Heathen pride. I'll break that pride."

Sarai said nothing more as they unchained her ankle from the post and led her with the slave collar chain out into the sunlight. She stopped in the doorway and breathed in the warm, living air. She looked about the little funeral crowd that now stood near the store and in the street. Ben pulled the new chain and Sarai, holding Summer against her, stepped forth on the wet soil. She followed behind Ben who carried the end of the chain. He led her out into the middle of the broad, melting street and started toward Silas's house before the onlookers. Sarai walked easily, erect, and at her full height.

"She walks like somebody important or a real queen,"

147

someone in the crowd said.

"She was somebody important among the Injuns," one of the onlookers said as he spat brown tobacco juice in the snow. "This is disgustin'. Let's get us a drank some'ers."

Ben jerked the chain, staggering Sarai onto her knees in the mud.

"Who the hell does he think he is? A damned conquering Caesar?" asked a leather-clad frontiersman.

"He's her uncle," the storekeeper said. "She's dangerous. Yes, sir, dangerous." Tell thought a minute. "But I don't think Ben's the conqueror. I think Ben Stone's got his hands full this time. Too full to turn loose of that chain."

Sarai rose from her muddy knees as he spoke and once again followed Ben at her own pace.

Chapter Twenty-One

Kane opened the door to the Land Records Office in Belknap. Behind him his muddy horse kicked out at the hitch rail horse nearest him. Kane's old buffalo robe coat thrown over the saddle nearly covered his animal. Two men stood at the counter and turned as Kane came in.

"Hey, Kane," said the clerk, "you back from your delivery to old Silas Stone."

"That's right," Kane said. "That's taken care of."

"Took twenty-five years, didn't it?" asked the clerk affably.

"That's right," Kane said. "Twenty-five years." But Kane had not waited through a blizzard and ridden through the mud flat plains to chat. "Say, Woody, has Logan been in here with the log books?"

"Logan ain't been in here with nothing, Kane," Woody said. "Either of you two seen Logan in town or at the Fort?"

The men Woody had addressed, shook their heads. "I don't think Logan's been here."

"Thanks, Woody," Kane said. "See you later."

Kane left the little jumbled firebox structure that held the treasured land records of the county.

W. Winn worked steadily over the barrel he was making in his small cooper's shop. Beyond him Kane saw Lou hanging her quilts out to air in the spring sunshine.

"Kane!" W said, looking up as he laid aside his hammer

149

and began working the stave with his skilled hands. "Lou! Kane's here."

"Don't quit for me," Kane said, dropping down on a barrel head.

"You look awful," Lou said, coming into the shade of the open shop. "I'll heat you some bath water." She turned to go to the house.

"Wait, Lou," Kane said. "Have you seen Logan?"

The man and wife looked at each other, knowing the danger to Logan or any man alone at the edge of the plains.

"Wasn't he to meet you on the way to Stone's Crossing?" asked Lou.

"He didn't," Kane said. "I thought maybe he'd come here with the Land Office logs first, but they haven't seen him."

Lou leaned back against a shed post, then sat slowly down on a keg beside it. W no longer worked his barrel.

"You think something has happened to Logan?" W asked.

"I don't know," Kane said. "It's not like Logan to break his word if he can help it."

Kane removed his sweat streaked hat and dropped it on the barrel next to his. He rubbed his burning eyes with the heels of his hands. Lou and W sat silently.

"Maybe the norther held him up," W speculated.

"Even if I could have missed him in the storm," Kane said, "he should have been here or at the Crossing long before this." Kane sat silently looking at his boots. "Somebody shot at us." His voice was very low. Kane cleared his throat. "Somebody tried to kill Sarai."

Lou leaned forward, putting her elbows on her knees and her hands over her mouth.

"You think Logan tried to kill the woman?" asked W.

"I don't know," Kane said. "I'm half crazy thinking he did or that something's happened to him, if he didn't."

"What makes you think Logan could kill Sarai?" asked Lou.

"He said she'd be better off dead, that her family would be better off," Kane said. "Then that night she tried to run off, Caleb Matthews from Mexia caught her and tried to kill her. But Logan was there and stopped him. Why was Logan there?"

"Maybe he followed her," W said.

"Maybe he followed her to kill her," Kane said.

"No, Kane," Lou said. "Logan stopped Caleb. If he'd wanted her dead, he could have let Caleb do the dirty deed."

"Maybe so," Kane said. "I want to believe that."

"But you don't," Lou said. "Why not, son? You love Logan like your own father."

Kane looked at Lou. "Rachel."

Ben transferred Sarai out to what Silas had called the old place the morning of the funeral. It was a small cabin not far from the river. The family had lived in it for a while before they built the fort. It was too small for so many, and they willingly abandoned it. Silas, however, had kept it up, had visited it from time to time.

Silas's old overseer, Jack, and his wife, Della, lived there now. They made a garden, kept a few chickens and pigs in the midst of the acres of Ben's cotton fields.

Jack had been boss for Silas's slaves. But Silas grew weary of cotton and slavery. As the years passed, he did not increase his workers. He cut back his farming, leased his land to other men, bought and sold land. One year, on his birthday, Silas freed his workers, gave them money and papers, a choice of going or staying. The younger ones left, but Jack and Della stayed to live out their lives on the old place and work for small wages.

Ben reined to a stop in the dirt yard. Jack came to the porch, raised his hand against the late morning sun.

"Get down, Mister Ben," he said. "Come inside by the fire."

"No time," Ben said abruptly. "This here's the woman from the Comanches. My father thought she was John's daughter, Sarai. His mind, of course, was going toward the end. But we've got her." Ben affected a resigned and honorable smile. "Pa signed some papers that make her our responsibility for now."

As he spoke, Ben dismounted and walked to Sarai's horse. The chain from her collar was locked through the saddle. He unlocked it, and pulled Sarai and Summer from the gray mare.

"She's dangerous, Jack. You'll have to keep an eye out."

Ben flipped the end of Sarai's chain around the porch post and locked it. He handed the key to Jack and walked back toward the horses.

"Keep her out of town, or I'll see you look for a new place to live, Jack. Pa's gone now, and I'm in charge. You know I'll keep my word. He wanted you and Della to stay here as long as you live. If you mind me, I'll keep his wishes just as long as I can." Jack's mouth tightened, but he said nothing to Ben Stone's threats. "See if you can sell this skinny Indian pony. Some of you people might use such an animal. It'll pay for the woman's feed a while."

Jack nodded, considering the mare. She was a running horse, not a plow horse, not a farm horse that Ben could use. She was not big or elegant enough for him to ride.

Ben's words recalled him from his observations. "Fix the woman a place in the shed. Wouldn't look right, a white woman in the same house as niggers. If she was a Stone, you'd have to live in the shed."

With that Ben mounted and started to ride away, but he stopped and turned back. He tossed a pocket knife to Jack who caught it neatly with both hands.

"Pa wanted you to have his knife," Ben said. "By the way, I hear you been horse racin' on the Sabbath again. That's a sin, Jack. Pa might have overlooked it. I won't. Not on my land. See it stops."

Ben left after that, riding away toward Murphytown.

Jack waited, then spat on the ground.

"Disgrace to the old man," he said. "Mean. Hard ass. Puttin' away his own flesh to live in a shed."

"Be quiet, Jack," Della said, aware of the white woman and child standing in the yard.

"She don't know what I said," said Jack.

"She sees plenty," said Della, moving closer to Sarai, looking at the clear blue eyes, seeing the animal quickness of her.

"Be careful there, woman," Jack said. "He say she dangerous."

"He say," the black woman said without moving away from Sarai. "He say. I be dangerous too if I have to stay around that man, let alone wear that iron necklace."

"Watch yourself," Jack said without much resolve. "Ain't that somethin', Silas Stone's blood granddaughter brought in chains to my door. What you reckon! Mr. Silas never went for no chains all the time I knowed him. No chains. No whips. 'Reason wif a man, Jack,' he told me. 'When you got to hit a man or a horse, he's beat you already.' Me young and strong and wantin' to pop heads wif any black man question me."

"It ain't right to chain up nothin' livin'," said Della quietly. "Let her go, Jack. She got a baby, and she ain't big enough to hurt nobody here. She ain't got no reason to hurt us. She's Silas Stone's blood. It's good blood."

"You crazy?" Jack said, looking at the key. "She's a wild Comanche. Besides Ben run us off this place just as soon as blink. Ben got all the difference."

"I won't go into town," Sarai said softly.

"How much talk you understand here, Miss Sarai?" asked Jack.

"I understood my uncle's bargain. I will stay here until time to go away. I will not hurt you. You were my grandfather's friend," answered Sarai. "Cut my hands loose."

Jack hesitated, gripping Silas's big pocket knife.

"You see, Miss, we po' folks. Ain't got no paper on this here land. Ain't got no money to get us another home. Too old to work hard now. Your uncle got heaps of money. He can run out most anybody here 'cause he owns paper on their land. He's got cash money, too. Wifout Mr. Silas to stop him, he do just what he please and holler Jesus told him to do it."

"Cut loose her hands," said Della impatiently. "We lost everything lots of times before."

Jack opened Silas's pocket knife and sawed through the binding cord. Sarai sat Summer on the porch as Jack unlocked her chain from the post.

"I ain't got no key to that neck piece," he said. "But I can bust off most of that chain if you promise not to kill us in our sleep."

"Do it," Sarai said. "I will not kill you."

Jack led Sarai down toward the little barn and his blacksmith tools. Carrying Summer, Della followed across the puddled yard. Snow patches still lay in the deep shadows against the side of the cabin and against the stick fence, but the air was mild, the beginning of spring.

" 'Spect you want this here end short so it don't fret you all the time, gettin' in your way," said Jack, as he searched out a chisel. "Kneel down here, and I'll strike a blow for freedom." Jack chuckled.

Sarai kneeled as Jack drew the chain across the anvil. Light fell through the broken roof onto her hair and face. The blue eyes never left Jack's face. He studied her face a minute, then drew back the hammer swiftly and drove it into the chisel, splitting the chain.

"I can still do it," he said, congratulating himself. "That arm ain't lost it."

Sarai rose to her feet, the chain dangling onto her chest. She held it with her left hand, jerked it gently against the neck ring.

Jack rustled around in a greasy tool box and pulled forth an open link of chain. Catching up the length of chain from the floor, he passed the open length through its loose end and the end Sarai held.

"Old slave trick," he chuckled. "Mister Ben comes, the dogs'll start barking. We fasten this chain here to the wall in that little shed yonder. You can go in there quick and put this link in and act like you chained up."

Sarai took the open link and turned it in her hand.

"You are afraid of Ben," she said. "But you honor

155

my grandfather. I will not forget who broke the chain Ben put on me."

Sarai looked out into the bright sunlight. The gray mare stood tied to the gate where Ben had left her. She pawed the muddy ground, eager to browse the sparse grass beyond her reach.

"The horse is mine," she said. "I raised her. She is worth more to me than a little money for food and clothes."

Sarai removed a wide silver bracelet from her wrist. "This will pay our keep till there is more."

Chapter Twenty-Two

Sarai's little house had been the slave cabin. It was a single pen log room with a fireplace at one end for heat. There was a broken wooden bed without a mattress, a table, and a chair with a missing rung.

"I can fix up that bed and chair just fine," said Jack. "We can put glass on the window. That fireplace draws good. Anyways it used to. Della's the best black woman to clean in Texas. Twice a week she went in and cleaned for Mr. Silas. Did all his laundry, too."

Jack took the chair and left.

"Come on, honey. We'll eat a bite of lunch 'fore we clean up this place fit for folks to live in," said Della.

She and Sarai went to the main cabin. It was white-washed inside and immaculate. Della still cooked on the hearth. Squirrel stew bubbled in the big iron kettle on the crane.

"Your grandma taught me to clean and to cook. She never took no short cuts, that woman. When I was plumb worn out, she was still going. 'Good spirits won't live in dirty places,' she'd say. I got so I was 'most as good about workin'. When the Indians killed her, it was like I lost my own mother. You're about her size. She was fair-skinned and light-haired, too."

Della talked as she sat mismatched plates and cups and utensils on the table. A heavy woman, Della moved with ease and grace of her own.

"Your mama's fair, too. Guess you come by it natural. I ain't seen her in long years."

Sarai listened intently, trying to catch all the words.

"My mother and father were killed with grandmother."

"Not your mama, child. Some Indian just knocked her in the head and rolled her down a little gully like he was tryin' to save her. We all hid out for two days in the river bed, scared them Indians'd come back, kill us all. Your mama was 'most crazy. She waited and waited for you to be found. I worked for her all that time. Finally your grandpa bought Johnny, but not you. Later when they found you, you wouldn't come back. Her sister got sick after that, and she went back to the old country we come from to take care of her. That's a long, long time ago now.

"Sit here," Della commanded Sarai. "Let me hold that little tike whilst you eat. I'm good feedin' little white babies. I fed you lots of times yourself."

Sarai stared at the bowl of stew for awhile and looked up at Della.

"You waitin' for the blessin', I 'spect. Lord Jesus, thank you for bringin' Miss Sarai and her child back to this house. Amen."

Still Sarai sat.

"What's the matter, child. It's good food. Ain't nothin' in there I won't eat myself. Nothin' that you ain't eat when you was small."

"I do not yet know the way of eating among you good," Sarai said simply. "I would like to know so I can eat better than Ben. Comanches are not ignorant savages. Comanches can learn new ways. It is good for a guest to learn the ways of the host."

" 'Sakes, child," Della said. "Just 'sakes. You goin' to make me watch my ways. It's a long time since I thought about teachin' behavior."

"You teach what you know. I watch, too. The People must have respect. Doctor's woman said dignity. Don't sit on the floor. Don't eat in bad way."

From then on Della became Sarai's teacher. They cleaned the cabin and washed and mended Sarai's clothes. They found some of Julia Stone's old clothes that fit Sarai perfectly. Every meal Della brought a tray of food to Sarai's house and set the table, pointing out the imperfections of the serving ware, telling the woman what to expect at a quality table, watching Sarai's efforts to perfect her actions.

"Eat slow," Della said. "Eat like a bird."

Della showed Sarai how to set a table, how to make a bed, how to cook white folk's food. Sarai showed Della how to make mesquite bread, how to find small wild potatoes on the plain. As the spring flowers covered the land, Sarai brought them into the house. They ornamented a jar on the well-scrubbed table.

Della and Sarai made soap from ash lye and lard, cooking it in a great kettle in the yard.

"White soap shows quality," said Della. "Show me a woman with old yella-orange soap, and I show you a trashy woman ever'time."

"Yucca is a soap," said Sarai. "It is white and soft. It does not want so much work."

Sarai went to the bags that once hung on her Spanish saddle. She showed Della the carefully wrapped roots that lathered into soap.

"Too easy, something wrong, child," Della said. "That's the way white folks think, and you got to start thinkin' white, if you expects to get past that Ben."

Sarai wrapped the soap and put it away.

"Sometimes white ain't so smart. Don't matter though when somebody else does the work."

"Lady don't never say 'ain't,' " Della said. "You can't talk like no field hand, child. But I ain't the one to teach you no talk."

At night after her dinner, Sarai sat at the table alone. Summer slept contentedly beneath the clean frayed quilt. Sarai looked at the table, spread her slender fingers on the rough wood. Moving restlessly around the walls, her eyes surveyed the empty cabin.

In one corner just under the bed sat a small chest. Sarai looked at it hard, saw it for the first time, and went to it. Lifting the lid, she discovered a lost world — the children's box. That was what her grandmother called it when it sat in the corner of her cabin.

Inside, Julia Stone, matriarch, teacher of the family, kept the slates and books necessary for frontier schooling. Sarai pulled the box into the light. Slowly, carefully, she took each item from it and laid it on the floor.

She remembered the lessons. She remembered Julia's admonition — "What you learn, a good education, nobody can take that away from you. It's your best friend on this earth."

Sarai almost moaned. But they had, she thought. Time and events had taken her memory of the letters and numbers and words. She rested her forehead on the lid of the chest.

"Get busy, Sarai-ah. Settle down and apply yourself," her grandmother's voice said as clearly as if she stood behind Sarai again.

Tears swam in Sarai's eyes, and she opened the small reader. Every night after that she sat with the box, turning slowly through each book, searching for the meaning of the marks on the page in her memory. Then at last, too tired for more, she lay down on the floor

160

and slept holding the chain of the iron slave collar.

As the ground dried out, Jack hitched a bald-faced mule to his plow and broke ground in the garden. The mule, full of spring and rested from the long winter, worked steadily under Jack's encouragements. Sarai and Summer sat on the porch step, watching the soil turn beneath the blade. Sarai's forehead knit into a frown as her eyes darted from the turning rich earth and plow to Jack and the mule. She leaned her chin on her hand. Pain showed in her narrowed eyes, and she winced each time Jack jerked the plow up at row's end and plunged it back into the fertile earth. Across the way other men, Ben's slaves, worked his fields.

"You got the stomach ache?" asked Della, as she picked up Summer who stretched up her arms to be lifted.

"No," said Sarai, as she continued to watch.

Della stepped behind Sarai to see what occupied her attention.

"What you see? Why, that's just old Jack makin' a garden! He done it ever' year. You used to ride the mule when you's little. After he plows, he'll plant, and one day there'll be food to eat, food for another year of life."

Sarai stood up and stepped onto the porch, turning her back on the plowing.

"Comanches don't tear the earth because it is sacred. Buffalo paw earth when they are ready to fight, makin' medicine, *puha*, power. White men get life from cutting the earth. My mind is full of many questions. I am weary of questions."

Sarai went away from Della toward the staked out mare. She caught up a handful of grass and offered it to the horse. After a few minutes she swung up on the warm back. She sat quietly with her hands crossed on her chest as the animal grazed. Sarai leaned forward, resting her cheek on the gray neck. Stroking the horse, she seemed to doze. Then her hands moved up to the rope on the mare's neck and loosened it. Suddenly Sarai was erect, and the rope lay on the ground. The mare flicked her tail, and they were gone across the flat land, running.

"What you think?" Della called to Jack who stood watching Sarai, growing smaller with the distance.

"I think if she gone, this mule ain't goin' to catch her back," he said. "That's a runnin' damn horse."

Chapter Twenty-Three

The wind felt good against Sarai's skin, like the breath of God blowing life back into her. As she rode, her mind began to lose the questions and confusion. This was what she wanted.

A rhythm had been broken in her, the rhythm of daylight and work and dark, of seasons, of twenty-five years. She had fallen out of the rhythm and waited like a dancer to catch the beat before stepping off again. Sarai was waiting too much — waiting for winter to come when the Comanches would again follow the buffalo into the Pease River country; waiting for something her grandfather rekindled in her heart; drifting among the white man's ways that were strange to her now; waiting for the dreams to have meaning. Sarai did not like the feeling within her — the restless, lonely feeling of hunger for change that had not yet come.

She controlled the horse easily with her weight and legs. In teaching the horses, she had learned to use her will, to temper and trust it. She loved the horse. Her Comanche heart exalted in the freedom it gave her. Sarai now needed to take control of her life again.

She was free — no chains held her. She could ride away across the prairie, live from the land, search until she finally found her sons. Sarai turned the mare west into the far emptiness and let her run. She could ride back at night and get Summer and be gone for good, rid forever of Ben Stone. Get Summer — and be gone now.

As she rode, Sarai began to hear the sound of guns behind her. Her heart pounded. She lay against the horse's neck, dodging the bullets that kicked up dust beside the running animal. She slid into a wash and rode down it through The People. Along its sides she saw the bloody bodies of Soldier's Coat, Elimah, Nobah sprawled in grizzly, vivid death. All the hurt rushed back, wave after wave of renewed sorrow. Nobah reached out to her. Reaching for him, she lost his hand and he fell away. There were others, hundreds of them.

Sarai rode faster, and ahead were her children — the two boys and little Summer. Sarai raised up. They waved. A barrage of bullets like swarming hornets passed her ears, and the children spun, fell before her eyes.

"No!"

Sarai threw herself from the horse and ran to them. And they were not there — only the red sand that ran through her scratched and bleeding hands.

As she lay on the earth, Sarai had had enough of the heart pain the Comanche life brought as the whites moved in and moved in on the wide land. She had had enough of worrying whether her men would return from raids on the settlements. Her sons would soon take the same road as their father and grandfather. It was a death road to Sarai. She had ridden down it. In her Comanche eyes it was far worse than death. It was a foolish, wasteful, impractical road that denied reality for pride. It was one thing to die for honor, another to die for stupidity.

There were better roads — the peace road. Sarai knew she could raise better horses than those the men risked their lives to take from the dirt farmers. Her horses could buy the blankets and goods the young men sacrificed their lives for. They need never again awake to screaming children and fire and the sound of guns.

Sarai loved Nobah. Her life was tied to his, but together they were of another time, the free time before soldiers and settlements. Time had caught them.

Sarai would have to change again. As once she had changed to being a Comanche, she must now change to being white again. She must change to save her children and bring them into the new time — just as she had brought them into life.

That was the chain that jerked Sarai back.

Sarai rose from the ground, threw her middle onto the horse, and pivoted up. She rode slowly back toward the old place, cooling the lathered horse, thinking what she must do to master this white world. Among the Comanches, physical courage, generosity of spirit, skill with horses, as well as her family gave her a place. She must find a key to unlock the white man's world.

Sarai rode across a wide, flat, hard-packed strip of land hidden by a roll of hills from the farmstead. The mare threw up her head, nostrils catching the smell of other horses, eyes focusing on a bit of red cloth flapping in the distance. Sarai looked around her. It was a race track.

She had raced many times at the forts and rendezvous. She saw in her mind the silver and gold coins and jewelry thrown on blankets. She saw the card players caressing stacks of coins, running their hands lovingly through their winnings. In the white world, money gave place. Ben had money. Sarai would have money.

Kane rode up on the rough outcrop. Below in the broken country lay the camp and Logan. He could see the wagons through the trees, but they were still too far away to be seen clearly. He did not see any horses, and no men moved about on the business of the camp.

He eased the big horse down the nearly vertical slope and rode closer to the survey camp. Kane kept to the trees, wanting to keep as much cover as possible until he knew the situation. His horse took the small stream quickly and without hesitation. Kane reined up on the far side, still covered by the trees, and waited. The birds along the creek sang their spring songs and flew purposefully, gathering their nesting materials. There was the sound of the creek, the wind in the trees. There were no human sounds.

Gently pulling the Sharps from its boot, Kane lifted himself from the saddle and stepped lightly onto the ground. Cautiously, he moved toward the wagons. The breeze freshened, carrying the faint scent of burned wood and carrion to Kane's nostrils. Kane sighed, knowing then the camp was lost; the men were lost. His heart tightened, enclosed by fingers of grief and pain. Logan. So this was how Logan ended.

Kane moved among the trees. He stepped over the remains of one of the men. He did not know him now. Even the clothes were torn and scattered. Kane walked slowly, in the open. Pages of carefully gathered survey logs riffled in the prairie breeze. Kane looked down, and then went on. He went from body to body, looking for Logan, looking for the identities of any of the men.

Near a wagon, he found the boy, Joe Ramsey. The animals had left a bit of hair that Kane recognized as the boy's. He found the cook. All along in his journey, Kane had counted. The boy made eleven, the cook twelve. There should have been one more. Kane turned about him, finding the perimeter of the fight. Someone must have crawled away. Kane began to walk again, circling around the edge of the camp, looking for the last body. His circle widened and widened until he was again at the creek and his horse. Still he had not found the body.

He stuffed the Sharps into the saddle boot and ducked under the horse's neck. The force of a blow caught him across the nose and between the eyes. Kane staggered and fell. The young Comanche waved to his companions. Together they tied the big Texian and threw him over his saddle.

Chapter Twenty-Four

Sarai brushed the curtain away from her window and looked out. Lifting her long skirt above her petticoat, she pulled her shirttail down within the waist band and watched Jack at the gate, talking to two strangers. He kept shaking his head, and the men in tall hats kept laughing. Summer giggled and peeked out of the bed covers. Sarai smiled and grabbed for her, rolling onto the bed. She kissed the child and held her close.

"Get up, sleepy head," she said.

"Get up," smiled Summer, hugging Sarai's neck.

Sarai lifted her daughter. "You little Comanche in a flour sack," she said, poking the faded imprint on the bleached sack that had become Summer's nightgown. "Maybe today we get some money."

Sarai dressed the child and directed her through the door. Across the bare yard Jack sat on the porch step, examining his tattered hat. Della stepped into the open doorway, and Summer started for her in a staggering run.

"Come on, precious," Della said. "I got you 'lasses and buckwheat cakes this morning."

Sarai sat down by Jack.

"Ain't my fault," he said. "I told them men Ben might have a hoppin' fit if they race here any more. They just laughed. White folks don't listen to no nigger. How'm I goin' to stop 'em?"

"They are racing today?" asked Sarai.

"That's right, first Sunday of the month, first week

168

of spring. I can't help it if this place is just half way between Stone's Crossing and Murphytown and made with that smooth place and shade trees to sit under and look out on it. Ain't me who put it here. Mr. Silas started the races, not me."

Jack was still talking as Sarai disappeared into the cabin.

Summer sat at the table under a dish towel bib eating pancakes. Her cheeks were streaked with molasses. The fork she held stuck straight up in her right fist on the table as she fished pieces of the cakes from the thick syrup with the fat fingers of her other hand.

"Good manners," Sarai said flatly.

Della turned around to see what Summer was doing.

"You little devil," she chuckled. "Teachin' is just wasted on you."

Della wet a cloth in the water bucket and washed the child briskly as she leaned over the food.

"Where's the silver bracelet?" Sarai asked.

"Behind the clock," said Della, looking up.

Sarai went to the clock and retrieved the piece of silver. She sat down at the head of the table and lay the bracelet on a napkin. She removed another bracelet and the heavy carved earrings from her ears.

"You look nekked without that silver in your ears," Della said. "What you up to?"

"I'm going to race the gray."

"Good Heavenly Father," Della said, throwing the wet towel on the table. "Pack yo' tools, Jack, Mr. Ben have us on the road by night! Your grandmother'll die."

"She's dead already," said Sarai, as she caught up the napkin and went outside.

"Stop her, Jack," Della called out.

"Stop her! Shoot!" said Jack. "She's hard-headed as

169

the old man hisself. Didn't take her no time to get *all white.*"

Sarai took the bucket of dishwater from the porch and started for the barn. Drawn by the unfolding events, Jack and Della followed with Summer. Sarai poured the water on the ground by the horse. She squatted and patted the water and dirt into a thick mud. She wiped the mud with her hands onto the horse's legs and neck and hips. The horse began to dance with excitement.

"Everybody likes to beat a tired out, ragged, old Indian pony. Don't matter, white or red, if it looks easy," Sarai said, rinsing her hands in the small amount of water left in the bucket.

Della shut her mouth tightly and said nothing.

Sarai rode the gray mare across the field and up the small hill above the track. She dismounted and walked the horse slowly under a tree. With the rein trailing across her shoulder and into her lap across the chain of Ben's collar, Sarai dismounted and sat down on her haunches. The mare stood, ears forward, forefeet together. With practiced eyes, they observed the racing scene, watched the running horses.

Below them, open carriages and wagons were drawn up in an informal grandstand above the track and in the protective shade of the trees and hill. There were ladies with parasols and ribboned hats and gentlemen in snug-fitting pants and fine calfskin boots. There were farmers and their wives and tow-headed children dressed in rougher clothing. There were a few blacks and Mexicans.

Sarai's eyes ran over the scene and came to rest on the circle of men near the horses. A short man with a great mustache occupied the center. He took money from the others, holding high a fist full of money, and calling for more bets. Sarai's eyes moved to the big sorrel that jumped nervously under its young black jockey. Farmers placed bets with the fat man. Their sons rode home-raised horses up and down in the nearby meadow.

The men moved slowly away, but in view of the finish. At last the horses made a dancing line. A young woman raised her 'kerchief in the air, then pulled it swiftly down. The horses ran. The spectators rose as one, craning to see the far turn. The galloping animals spun dirt into the air and headed flat out for home. The sorrel easily won. The money changed hands.

His black rider led the sorrel away, down to the river to cool and drink. Sarai tied her mare and walked along the ridge and down to the water. Watching the horse drink, she washed her face and hands and let the crowd of jubilant boys drift away. The jockey-groom wiped the sorrel with linen rags.

"He runs good," Sarai said.

The boy looked up at the ragged woman.

"Better than good," he said. "This hoss'll beat anything in Texas. He born to run. Judge Garrett bought him for one thing . . . win."

"Can anyone run horses here?" asked Sarai.

"Anyone fool enough," answered the jockey. "Got to qualify for the big race and got to have the throw-down."

"What is 'qualify?' "

"Means you got to have a horse good enough to win a race, so if you get in the big race, it'll be interestin', and so you don't get a shot at the prize wifout havin' been seen befo'," said the youngster.

"And 'throw-down.' What is 'throw-down?' "

171

"Money. You throw down on the bet," he said.

"Only money?"

"No," the jockey said. "They bets other things, too. Watches and rings and carriages, and land sometimes."

Sarai walked slowly back up the hill. There were other races, between the farmers, between the gentlemen. The morning moved lazily down toward noon. At midday, there was a long break. Hampers of food came out — rich food in the carriages, plainer fare from the wagons. Enjoying the early spring day, the people ate leisurely. Sarai watched. A card game started under a mesquite. Further away horseshoes clanked around metal stobs and bedded on the sweet-smelling earth. Further down, some Germans threw silver dollars — closest man takes all.

After the nooning, the races began again. Sarai swung up on the mare and rode down among the gathering. She bet the earrings and bracelets against a small gold piece, some silver, a few paper notes. She squeaked by the farm horses.

The next race was better stock. She bet the paper. The muddy little gray started slow and failed among the big, long-legged horses. Sarai lost the paper to a fiery bay ridden by his owner.

Afterward she walked the mare, stroking her nose and talking to her. They returned to the hill and waited and watched more races. At last the fighting sorrel was brought up again. The big men with the big horses gathered.

"Final race, folks," the little fat man called out. "Last chance. Yancey's bay against my sorrel. Takin' your money, gents."

"I would bet this," Sarai said softly among the men's voices.

"On the sorrel?" the rotund little Judge asked.

"On the gray mare," she said.

"Who's she?" Judge Garrett quietly asked a by-stander.

"The one who's goin' to beat you, mister," Sarai said.

Judge Garrett laughed, studying the ragged woman.

"You must be Silas Stone's Comanche. Put up that Indian pony and you're in."

Sarai thought, then nodded.

"Glad to take your money, ma'am." The judge touched his hat. The other men laughed.

"All right, boys. Show some courage. Let's get some more horses and money in here! Makes life more interesting. Come on, Cyrus, run that gelding of yours."

Cyrus P. Peabody shook his head.

"Race is between your's and Yancey's horses. Rest of us are out-classed. I don't throw money away, Judge. A banker can't afford to."

"Well, now, Yancey, let's see what you got to top this lady's bracelets and do-dads," said the judge.

"I got a quarter-section of cotton land down the river and $500 in gold," said Yancey.

The crowd shuffled at the high stakes.

"Hell, boy. You're gettin' serious now," said the judge. "But I am prepared to wager, in addition to my carriage. . . ."

The judge dropped a sack of coins, a stack of crisp bills, as well as a folded deed on the table beside Yancey's wager and Sarai's bracelets and earrings.

Yancey opened the judge's deed and then dropped it back on the table.

"Winner takes all?" the judge asked.

Yancey nodded.

"Race is down to that pen, around, across the slope

173

there, and back. No hitting or bumping the other fella's horse," said the starter, striving for attention. "May the best man win."

"Winner takes all," Sarai said, and moved away from the circle of men while they concluded their bets. She untied the mare, and she stepped onto a crate to mount heavily up. Both mare and woman seemed small and exhausted. They stood silently near the two rearing champions. The black jockey's hands were raw from holding rein on Judge Garrett's sorrel. The bay jerked his holder from the ground and tossed his shapely head.

At last the bettors moved off. The judge walked happily toward his handsome carriage among his jovial companions.

"I been waitin' for this," he said. "I been waitin' for this, three years."

The judge stopped for a few minutes and squinted at the woman and her horse, considering. He shook his head.

"Probably that horse is the only thing she owns," he said. "Shame. Ben wouldn't let her have a dime. I won't accept her things, of course."

"You know, Judge," said his friend, Cyrus P. Peabody, with his hands thrust deeply into his pockets, "I don't know if you were smart to let that gal in the race. It's just too good. Have you watched her? She gets on from the right just like a Comanche. No whip. No saddle. She's carrying less weight than either rider out there. If I'm not mistaken, she's up on a horse she's raised and trained and knows. That mud and her raggedy clothes are deceiving us like blind fools. On top of all that, she's Silas Stone's granddaughter. I've the strangest feeling we're going to be walking home."

Sarai loosened the bright shawl that hid the iron slave

collar. The chain fell across her chest as she tied the shawl around her waist. She wanted to feel the loathsome thing, her constant companion in the time since her grandfather's death. The black jockey looked at her as he fought the horse. Yancey caught a stirrup and threw himself aboard the bay.

"Ready," the starter called out.

The gray's ears shot up.

"Get set," he said.

Sarai felt the mare plant her back feet.

"Yo!"

The gray burst forth with Sarai against her neck, yelling. They ran in pure joy, away from the sorrel, away from the bay, away from Ben's tyranny.

"What in hell," said the judge, standing in his carriage. "That horse never got off like that before. Use the whip, Ustus! Hit that damned horse, or I'll sell you as a pair!"

The sorrel's jockey laid into the heavy rump and the horse leaped forward, striding evenly toward the gray. The bay's ears went flat as Yancey applied his whip. The big horses gained on the flat, consuming ground with each long stride. The slender legs of the gray reached out. Still the others stayed, gained on her.

Nearing the turn, the big horses blocked the gray, held her between them. Sarai could not see or stretch out her arms. The smell of men and animals was in her nostrils. The curses and coaxes filled her ears as the men fought through her at each other's horse.

"Give way," Yancey shouted at Garrett's jockey.

"Nawh, sir," the black youth said. "This here's Judge Garrett's hoss. It don't give way to nobody, sir."

The boy was talking, but not listening to himself as he concentrated on the race.

The bay blew hard under the heavy weight of Yancey,

taking the turn a fraction late. It was nothing more
than a breath really, but the bay fanned his broad rump
into the sorrel, tangling back feet with red.

Sarai felt it. Saw the opening. Cut across it. The bay's
hot breath burst over her cheek and ear as she shot
past. She leaned low on the mare's neck. The damnable
chain fell cold on her hands. She stretched her arms
forward along the gray's neck.

They were flying. The sounds of heaving breath from
the larger horses and pounding hoofs gave way to silence
as the little gray flew on toward the red flannel flag.
Sarai saw it, and then they were gone by, floating, coast-
ing toward a stop long beyond.

Sarai straightened up. Her mud covered pony slowed
into an easy canter. They made a wide circle back toward
the screaming crowd. Sarai smiled a small, private smile
as the mare fell into her slow, easy trot. The gray stopped
obediently before the judge and nudged the judge's
stomped top hat on the ground.

"I knew it," he said, red-faced. "In my heart, I knew
I shouldn't let you in. The race was between young
Yancey and me for the cotton land. That's all it was
for. And you took it for a silver bracelet and an Indian
pony I wouldn't have. Hot damn Judge Garrett for a
fool."

"That what you're running for next, Judge?" someone
laughed from the crowd of men.

"Shoot, son, I won that today by a landslide," Garrett
said, beginning to laugh at himself. "By crackers, boys,
she doesn't need any lawyer or banker for a trustee.
And she damn sure ain't feeble-minded like Ben said.
She's plenty sharp . . . sharp as Silas said."

"Pay the lady," Yancey said, dropping from the foam-
flecked bay and handing the reins to his groom.

"Well, dear lady," said the little judge, "we can hand over the pot and our deeds quite easily. But I shall greatly miss my carriage, and my wife and daughter will give me no peace for that loss, if they and their guest must ride home in a farm wagon."

The crowd laughed.

"You may send the carriage to me tomorrow," Sarai said. "At the Old Place, not at Ben's."

The judge chuckled.

"By crackers, Silas would be proud of you. You deal like a gentleman. And you've got both your eyes open, too." The judge's small eyes narrowed in his ruddy cheeks. "What's that about your neck, child?" He reached out and caught the length of chain. "Cyrus, let's find some keys and get this monstrosity off the woman."

Sarai's hand closed over his.

"No," she said softly. "He who put it there must take it away."

Judge Garrett studied the woman.

"Eyes open, like I said. Gather your loot, then. But remember, we'll be watchin' for you next time."

"Next time maybe I can afford to lose . . . a little," Sarai said, taking the napkin with the bracelets and earrings and putting it inside her shirt. She looked at the tidy stack of deeds. "This is land?" she asked. "I now own the land?"

"That's right. Prettiest little piece of bottom land I ever saw, and mine joining it, too," the judge said wistfully.

"Nobody can run me or my people away from it?"

"That's correct. Nobody. Not so long as you pay your taxes and don't mortgage it," the judge said.

"Pay taxes. Do not mortgage," she said softly.

Sarai did not understand the words, the foreign concepts they represented, so she said no more. Wariness was a trait she learned early. So far among the whites, she saw no reason to drop it. Revealing her ignorance too quickly, too publicly only invited attack. She would pick her time. But she knew this game was much trickier than the simple horse race that had won her the land and money.

A Comanche believed that if you could not keep a horse or blanket, it was not yours. Their few possessions were ruled by that belief. Their raids into the settlements only applied the premise. They were not thieves in their own eyes, but merely players in an ongoing contest in which all things remained prizes. With the white man keeping was more complex than getting. It was not merely a matter of strength or of cleverness or of possession. The game was played more elaborately with words and papers, and it was a game just as deadly, too.

It all lay there in the folded pieces of paper. Sarai opened the top deed and looked at the fancy border, the florid scrolls and writing. On that Sunday, she ran headlong into a whole new level of learning and possessing and surviving. Inside, her heart raced. A cold fear filled her because she did not know, did not understand this paper world.

She wanted to run away even as she refolded the paper. Yet she wanted the papers. Her hand caressed them like a bird that might fly away. Jack and Della taught her the importance of paper to freedom among the whites. Because they had no paper on the land, Ben could run them away. Because they had a paper from Silas, he could not sell them or put a chain around their necks again. Sarai started to put the paper in her shirt.

"Wait up," said the banker, Cyrus P. Peabody. "She'll need your transfer signatures."

Sarai watched the men perform the paper ceremony, then Cyrus P. offered her the pencil and pointed at a line.

"Sign here," he said.

Sarai looked into his pink, clean-shaven face.

"Your mark will do," he said quietly, just to her.

Sarai took the pencil awkwardly. Slowly she drew a curving line above the printed line. She darkened a triangle at the right end making an angular head and gave the pencil back. It was the sign of the snake, the sign for Comanches in the language of the plains. Among the whites it was the sign of the fall from innocence and the beginning of knowledge.

Chapter Twenty-Five

Kane sniffed and opened one aching eye.

"Geez us, damn," he said.

The broken nose throbbed. The redness and swelling extended under his eyes.

"That was a real nice rescue attempt you made," Logan said.

"Logan!" Kane almost shouted. "Logan, I could damn near kiss your ugly face." Not only was Logan alive, but he could not have fired the shot at Sarai.

"You think a bunch of semi-savage Injuns could kill me, son?" Logan asked. Kane nodded.

"Well, they didn't." Logan thought a minute. "But they damn near did. What took you so long to get here?"

"Hell," said Kane, "I didn't know I was expected. I just wondered why you didn't show up and came looking."

"The kid didn't make it, then?" asked Logan.

"If you mean Ramsey, I found enough of him under one of the wagons to know him," said Kane. "What do you mean, didn't make it?"

"Nobah sent him for you," Logan said.

"Why?" asked Kane.

"He wants her back. Figured you'd trade her for me," Logan said.

"Logan," Kane said, "I owe you an apology."

"You didn't know about the trade," Logan said.

"No," Kane said, "I didn't. But what I'm apologizing for is not trusting you. Someone took a shot at the woman and me. After the business with you being there to catch Caleb Matthews, and you not showing up in Belknap, I thought maybe you tried to kill her."

"If I'd tried," Logan said matter of factly, "she'd be dead."

"I guess I know that too," Kane said. "Somehow, Logan, Rachel's all tangled up in this. I've been scared of you since Rachel died."

Logan sat quietly looking at the ground.

"I reckon I've been scared of myself, too. Why in hell did I shoot her? I've asked myself that a million times. I could have gone to her and picked her up and held her and tried to make things better, but I aimed and fired without a thought." Logan shook his head. "I don't know why I done it. Seein' the baby dead, her killin' him . . . maybe I thought I was protecting the child. But I think. . . ." Logan paused. He cleared his throat and looked earnestly at Kane. "I think I just couldn't stand her pain any more. I made it easy on myself."

"Easy, hell!" Kane said. "I've been around you almost every day for twenty-five years. You've carried Rachel's pain every one of them days."

"Maybe so. Mostly I've been burdened by my own frailty. Man's a frail thing. That's a hard fact. I just couldn't make it right for Rachel. I couldn't do it. But this Sarai Stone is a different kind of woman, a whole different deal from Rachel. She ain't broke up inside."

Logan stopped talking and looked around.

"Ain't this a mess? Well, we got it made now. Between us we can whip their tails and get the hell out of here."

Kane looked at Logan. He was hollow-eyed. A stubble beard covered his cheeks. His neck was burned raw where a rawhide rope held him. His clothes were ripped and torn and filthy. His hands were tied across his stomach. A lance shaft ran between his elbows and across his back.

"This rig's a bitch to sleep in," he said apologetically.

"You figure we've got 'em outnumbered?" Kane asked.

"That's right," Logan said. "But I got one more job when we've finished 'em. I aim to kick hell out of a dog."

"What dog?" Kane said.

"That big son-of-a-bitch that comes by here ever' so often and lifts his leg?" Logan said.

Kane laughed and grimaced at the pain that shot through his head.

"Shoot, Logan. For a minute there I thought we were in trouble."

"Trouble, hell! It's these puny Indians that's in trouble, if they only knew it," Logan said. "I aim to inform them directly. Funnin' aside, Kane, Nobah. . . ."

Logan did not get his words out before a handful of Comanche bucks came around the teepee side. They jerked Kane up and carried and dragged him toward the shade arbor where Nobah lay. They dropped Kane unceremoniously in front of their leader.

The Comanche watched Kane right himself. He did not offer to help nor did he speak.

Kane's nose ran blood onto his shirt front. He squinted through the pain and swelling at the Comanche who leaned against a back rest. There was no paint on his fine features, but ornaments hung from his ears and neck. His chest was bare and hard, the color of rich red earth. For an instant, the picture of Sarai's fair skin against the Indian's darted through Kane's mind. Quickly he pulled himself back, concentrating on the scars of many battles on Nobah's chest and arms. His swollen eyes did not miss the wrapping around Nobah's ribs that covered a recent wound.

"You may have Logan back when I have the woman," said Nobah. "That is simple enough even for a white man to comprehend. You have taken my family, and I want them back. My wife, my sons, my daughter . . . my family. That simple."

Kane looked at the chief. "That's a big trade for just Logan. Why would I go to all that trouble?"

"Because Logan is your father, your family," said Nobah.

Kane thought about Nobah's words. The Indian knew his way around and did not miss anything. Logan was his father and brother and mother and friend. Kane knew Logan's grief and his courage and his care, as well as he knew his own.

"She's with her grandfather and living well. Maybe she does not want to come back," Kane said.

"She will tell me herself, or you will not get Logan," Nobah said.

"The little girl is with her, but I have no knowledge of your sons," Kane said.

"You bring the woman and the little girl to me," Nobah said. "Then, you may seek my sons as you sought her. I will keep Logan until I am satisfied."

Chapter Twenty-Six

When Sarai returned to the farmstead, she wore the silver bracelets, and the heavy earrings hung from her ears. The gray horse fairly danced under the winnings held in Judge Garrett's picnic napkin.

Della stood waiting on the porch with Summer in her arms. She looked closely at Sarai and slowly a smile broke over her broad face revealing white teeth with a small gap between the two in front.

"Jack, she's wearin' the earrings. Jack, get out here!"

Jack limped out onto the porch, but Della was down in the yard, already handing Summer up to Sarai and taking the winnings bundle. Sarai cantered the pony around the yard and down to the creek. Leaving Summer on the horse, she dismounted and washed the mud from the mare while she drank. Later they went back through the spring twilight to the Old Place.

Jack and Della sat on the porch analyzing the contents of the napkin as Sarai, the child, and the horse returned.

"Child, you are rich!" said Jack. "This here's sincere money. Hm. Hm."

"Too easy," Della pouted, dampening her own pleasure with the necessary remark. "Come too easy, too quick. Mess of trouble if you ain't careful there."

"Not too easy," said Sarai. "Took a long time to raise this horse and to learn the ways of running. Things must happen quick to catch me up with this white world."

Sarai dropped down by the outspread bundle with

Summer in her lap. She brought the deeds forth from her black shirt.

"We have paper now. Ben cannot throw us away."

She offered the deeds to Jack who took them carefully and opened one with his finger tips.

"Read it to me," Sarai said.

Jack shook his gray head. "You know I can't read, Miss Sarai."

Sarai's forehead drew together in a frown. She looked at Della.

"Don't you looka here at me," Della said softly. "Black folks ain't allowed to read. Anybody teach 'em go to jail."

"Why?"

" 'Cause we weren't free," Jack said, "and somebody else do our thinkin' fer us anyway. Don't want us findin' out things and thinkin' fer ourselves."

Sarai looked at her mentors in the dim light. She sensed their shame at their impotence before the paper, at their vulnerability through ignorance of the words. In her mind where she catalogued the other injustices against the weak, Sarai put the law against reading. What power this ability to understand the crooked little lines must give! How closely the white men guarded it! Sarai would read and write her name and other words. Her children would read and write, she had decided.

"We have land now . . . cotton land once belonging to a man called Yancey and some land joining it that belonged to Judge Garrett. We must pay taxes and not mortgage it to keep it. No one can tell us to leave if we do those things," Sarai said.

"You won Yancey's bottom land?" whispered Jack. "Oh Lord, now we responsible. Lord. Lord."

"Quit you' Lord, Lord," said Della. "Lord give this

woman good land, and you whimpering for some little old scraggly piece of sandy land. Shame on you. You know how to work good land. Take care of it. You done it before."

"Good land need work," said Jack. "If I could work good any more, you think I be sittin' here. I'm a old man, woman, turned out 'cause I ain't no good."

"Hush that up," said Della. "God don't make no mistakes. It's good land for a purpose, and there's a way provided."

"Tomorrow we will have a carriage and team, too," Sarai said.

"Oh Lord," said Della.

Jack sat back against the wall. "Whose carriage, Miss Sarai?"

"Judge Garrett's."

"Oh Lord, Lord," said Della.

"Hush that up, woman," Jack said. "That's a mighty fine outfit. Come from back East by boat. We got to figure out what to do . . . what Mr. Silas do."

The women waited for Jack to think.

"I best study this out a spell longer," he said, getting up. "But one thing fo' sure, land an' what she do, the most important thing."

"Jack," Sarai said to the old man, "tomorrow Ben will take this chain off me. When I am free of it, we must be smarter than Ben, or he will look big, and we will seem small. He might get power over us again. I know little of white men, except they give way to money and hold it close. It is not so with the Comanches . . . a man is respected for his deeds and character. A man is big as he shares with his people."

"It's that way with quality folks ever'where," Della said. "Ben ain't even much of a white man 'cept for what he holds over folks and scares out of them. Don't take him for no example."

"I will be better than Ben, not like him. I will be like my grandfather," said Sarai.

She took Summer and walked to her cabin, leaving the winnings for Della to put away.

Kane nodded to Logan who stood bound beside Nobah. The Indian was pale and weak. Logan looked worse, but kept up his feisty defiant ways.

"Bring me a steak, Kane. Two inches thick and three foot around. These damn Indians can't cook nothing that sticks to a man's ribs." Logan grinned crookedly. " 'Seein' you, son."

"You damn right," Kane said under his breath as he turned the horse toward the Texas settlements.

Ben Stone dropped the reins over the hitch post in front of Tell's general store. He caught heavily at the rail and pulled himself up the steps. Layers of dust coated his black broadcloth suit. A day's growth of whiskers covered his face. Ben turned the door knob slowly and stepped inside.

" 'Morning, Ben," Tell called out cheerfully. The other men, bright and fresh with the new day, sat about the stove and coffee pot in the store. They spoke and nodded.

Ben mumbled a return greeting of sorts.

"Why, Ben, if you was a drinkin' man, I'd say you had a drop too much," said Tell.

"Say what you like," grumbled Ben, "I'm too tired to resist you. This is the last time I ever go to Austin. I'm too old, and it's too far away. How 'bout a cup of that hot coffee to get me home?"

187

Tell filled a thick crockery mug and passed it over to Ben.

"What's the talk down there?" one of the loafers asked.

"War and Indians," Ben said brusquely. "Ain't no useful talk out of anybody. War and Indians. Nobody's talkin' money."

Tell laughed with the other men. "Reckon all the money talk's up here," he said.

"How's that?" Ben asked, swallowing the burning brew.

"Your niece came into some money yesterday," Tell said, giggling.

"My niece?" Ben sat the cup on the counter and narrowed down on the storekeep. "What money?"

The men in the store became suddenly still at Ben's deadly tone.

"I said, what money, Tell."

"Why, Ben," the storekeeper swallowed, empty now of jokes and fun, "your niece . . . she won the last race. That little gray of hers took the day. Cleaned out Judge Garrett and. . . ."

"I told that damned nigger Jack no more races. Not on my place. I warned him. I'll run that sorry, worthless, old black nigger out of Texas. Played on my sympathy for the last time."

Ben spit the venomous words into the quiet air.

"Won't do you much good, Ben," Charlie Legg said with some pleasure. "She won Yancey's bottom land right alongside the Judge's. Her name's on the deed, and I figure she's goin' to remember Jack and Della just like Silas wanted."

"Silas is dead," Ben said, looking into the other man's eyes. "That place belongs to me now. What I say goes. They won't be livin' on my land, none of 'em. And between the three of them, they don't have the sand or sense to run or keep the bottom land."

"I don't know, Ben," one of the men said thoughtfully. "If you'd seen her yesterday, you might think different. She was plenty smart and cool. Plenty stony, too. Bet her life in a way running under them big horses. She's a lot like Silas."

"She's an ignorant, heathen woman. A sinner before God. A savage. An animal, not even human. She won't get away with it. She won't."

Ben spoke through gritted teeth.

He left the store, but he did not go home for a shave or nap. He went straight to the sheriff's office.

Chapter Twenty-Seven

Jack and Della sat on the seat of the wagon as Sarai knocked at the door. While she waited, Sarai studied that door out of which she had once been cast. When it opened, she did not find Ben. Jane answered. She stared at Sarai, who stood straight and calm before the door, asking for her uncle.

"He sent word he's back from Austin, but he's gone to his office," said a startled Jane as she kept the door between her and Sarai. "It's in town. Across from Tell's store. You'll find him there, not here. There." Jane spoke a little loudly and gestured toward town. "There. That away. ¿Comprende?"

"I understand," said Sarai. "But I left something of mine in this house. My book."

"That's a child's book," said Jane.

"It is *my* book. Silas gave it to me."

"Shoot!" Jane started to close the door, but Sarai stretched out her hand, stopping it. "It's simple-minded for a grown-up woman to want a baby book. I ain't sure where it is anyway."

"I know where I left it," Sarai said, stepping forward.

"It ain't there now. I'd feel a fool lookin' for it," said Jane quickly, resisting Sarai's pressure on the door.

"I would feel a fool pushing a door against someone who asks for such a little thing," Sarai said, dropping her pressure.

"All right. All right. Come on in. I guess it's safe

enough. At least, you can talk now. But Ben won't like this."

Jane opened the door.

"Ben won't like this one bit."

"I will soon deal with Ben."

Sarai unwrapped the Mexican shawl from her throat as she stepped inside, revealing the iron collar. Jane almost gasped, but put her hand over her mouth before the sound escaped. She had seen Ben lead Sarai through the streets, had seen the collar on her neck as Ben fastened her to a ring in the fireplace after Silas's funeral. But Sarai was an animal then, not a woman who talked to her. Jane turned away quickly, confused by the sudden rush of her thoughts against Ben — the way he threw the woman and child out into the storm, the way he dragged her and chained her, the way he left her with the old slaves just to survive. Sarai's mother ought to know, she thought. Jane suddenly wondered if Lady Stone even knew that Sarai was back. Someone ought to write to her.

Sarai followed Jane through the house to Silas's room. She looked about.

"It's in the wardrobe, I think," Jane said, opening the wide walnut door. Silas's clothes hung neatly where he'd left them. "Ben won't wear Silas's clothes. I can't see why not. They're all good as new, and I can take up the legs easy enough. But Ben won't have it. Superstitious or something. Wants 'em give away. Here it is," Jane said, retrieving the book from the depths of the old chest. As she turned around, the look of sadness in Sarai's eyes caused her to stop. "I didn't reckon you knew Silas well enough to be grieved at my words."

"Silas was with me all the time when I was with

191

the Comanches, especially when I was little. The men he sent kept him before me as I grew. I was not alone while Silas lived." Sarai took the offered book and started to leave.

"Wait. He was good to me, too, even after that Rachel business," said Jane impulsively, spurred by sudden resentment against Ben. "There's something else."

She went to the desk.

"I found this the other day. Ben don't know about it. It's got your name on it. Silas meant it for you."

She gave Sarai the letter Silas had written before he died.

"Go on now. I got things to do. Close the door behind you. This ain't no teepee," she said softly.

Jane did not follow Sarai to the door. She went into the kitchen. When she heard the front door close, she sat down at the table and rested her face in her hands.

Outside Sarai put her book and letter into her saddle bags.

"It gets late," she said to Jack. "You go on toward the farm. I will catch you after Ben takes this off." She wrapped the scarf again around her throat.

"That Ben may be bad," said Jack, looking over the smooth rumps of the new mules.

"I will deal with that Ben," said Sarai, and smiled at her friends. "I will not be long."

Sarai watched the wagon off down the road, then pressed the mare's side gently with her heel. She rode slowly down the dirt road. A dog ran out from behind a picket fence. The little gray turned her head and pricked up her ears, but did not shy. She kicked out one back foot for the sake of kicking more than for the sake of hitting.

A woman, hanging clothes on a rope line stopped,

arms suspended in mid air as she watched Sarai pass. As Sarai went toward town, people came out of their houses, following the white Comanche to her destination. Some ran ahead, knocking on doors, alerting friends to the pending event.

They were not different, Sarai thought, from the Comanches who came out of their teepees to hear the news and see for themselves the curious happening. Some of these white people even reminded Sarai of Comanches — the man with the big belly of Far Elk; the woman scurrying after a shirt blown loose by the wind of Earnest Woman.

Della reached out and caught the reins. "Jack, you stop here. I ain't goin' off an' leave that child to Ben."

"What you goin' to do, woman?" said Jack. "She's plum out on her own fer as our help go."

"Well," said Della, lifting her head, stretching to see down the road after Sarai, "well, we can wait back where the road comes out. Just be there fer her."

Jack shook his head but quickly turned the team. He brought them to a smooth stop at the end of the town road.

He smiled to himself. "I sure am glad you a hard woman, Della."

By the time Sarai reached the board walks and buildings of town, Ben stood with his hands in his pockets, waiting. She stopped in front of him. Neither spoke for a long while.

"Uncle," Sarai said, "we have left your farm. And I would have your iron collar off my neck."

Ben did not move but studied Sarai as she pulled off the bright scarf from her worn black shirt and

193

dropped it over the mare's withers.

"You think you are smart, don't you, Missy?" he said. "Think you've got me just where you want me. Well, you don't."

His cold eyes traveled past Sarai to the onlookers gathered across the street and behind picket fences.

"Not you," Ben said softly. "It's one thing to get land, another to keep it. Takes stay. No Indian ever born has it. Fight and run away, that's Indian. Not me, woman, I'm steady on. I keep coming. You'll learn that. You're just a gambler, a whore, a Comanche concubine. You ain't even fit to walk amongst decent folks."

"Uncle, calling me a blue jay or a sparrow will not make me fly. Your words are empty. They have meaning only for your bitter heart. Do you have the key?"

Ben looked down at the boards he stood on, turning the key in his pocket, delaying the bitter action of unlocking the slave ring, of being bested before the town. The key became hot in his hand as he pressed it. "Get down."

Sarai stepped onto the hitching rail, and then the walk. She waited in front of Ben, mocking the heavy collar and Ben's massive size with her small, slight figure. Her eyes never left Ben's face. Ben set his jaw, pushed his lower lip forward, and brought forth the key. His fist caught the iron ring and jerked Sarai to him. He thrust the key into the collar and felt her warm pulse against his hand. Blue eyes met and held blue eyes.

"You have not won yet. Not by a damn sight. I keep comin' till I win," Ben said. Then he looked down and turned the key. He stepped away, through the office door. Sarai reached up and spread the collar open.

Like smoke, Sarai was on the horse. Holding the slave collar high over her head, she rode through the crowd that parted before the horse and rider, and cantered leisurely out of town.

"Looks like things are catching up with old Ben," Charlie Legg said to Tell, and spat in the street. "Sometimes nature herself do conspire and converge upon a man."

"Here she comes," Della said straining up from the wagon seat. Her hand fell on Jack's old leg, and she gripped it hard. "Here she comes."

Just past the blacksmith shop, Sarai whirled the horse and ran her hard back towards the office. She skidded the mare into a rearing stance and threw the iron collar through the big glass window with Ben Stone's name in gold letters.

Sarai shouted out a triumphal challenge, a war cry — a Comanche victorious over her foe.

Red with anger, Ben charged to the broken window. Just as quickly as she came, Sarai was gone, cantering down the dirt road, tasting the sweet wind of freedom.

Ben looked at the ugly iron laying on the floor amid the shards of glass. He sat down and put his head in his hands.

"It is not over yet, Missy. Not by a damn shot."

Chapter Twenty-Eight

After hearing the story, Kane left Stone's Crossing with a certain satisfaction, knowing that Sarai had beaten Ben at his own game. Had shoved his damned chains and slave collar back in his face. Logan was right. This woman was different — nothing was broken inside of her. Finding Yancey's place would be easy.

He found the beginnings of a homestead under the old pecan trees along the river. Jack and the young black man, Amos, and the mules were in the fields. Della had a wash pot going and clothes flapping in the prairie wind. She dropped peeled potatoes into an iron kettle that hung from a chain and tripod over a fire.

Kane swung down near the canvas covered wagon.

" 'Day to you," he said to Della, who watched him closely but said nothing. "I'm looking for Sarai Stone. This is her place?"

"You ain't no gypsy are you?" asked Della.

"No, I'm not a gypsy," Kane said. "At least not much any more."

Della kept peeling potatoes, preoccupied with her thoughts.

"Are there gypsies in the neighborhood?" asked Kane.

"Whole mess of 'em down there." Della gestured over her shoulder with the knife. "Thieves is what they ought to be called. That's what they are. Stole all my chickens like that." Della snapped her fingers. "Jack's dogs never made a whimper, and them gypsies had my chickens 'fore daylight and gone. Lord, it's a wonder they ain't stole off this child and sold her."

Kane reached down and picked up Summer.

"You're pretty enough to steal," he said. "Prettier even than the last time we met."

"How you know that child?" asked Della, looking up suspiciously from her work.

"Oh, we're old friends." Kane tossed Summer giggling into the air. Then holding her close to him, he said, "I brought her and her mother to Stone's Crossing. Now I need to find Sarai Stone."

"She went off to town after getting my chickens back and that yella wagon from them gypsies."

Kane looked where Della pointed with the knife. A painted yellow gypsy wagon was parked under the trees. Five crates of chickens were tied to the sides in clear view of the ever watchful eyes of Della. "They's just innocents messin' with Miss Sarai. That's a fact." She chuckled, thinking of Sarai and the gypsies.

"Murphytown?" asked Kane.

"That's right. Uh-huh. Gone to learn to write her name, she said."

Sarai rode the gray mare among the houses off the main street of Murphytown. A dog barked at her from the taut length of chain that held him captive to a white house. Some of the houses were big and fine, made of brick and stone with tall columns along the wide porches, others small and shabby with dirty naked children playing in the dirt yards. Some houses had gardens. Women took down clothes from their wash lines and stared at Sarai as she stared at them.

She found the school with children darting down the steps toward home. The littlest children carried slates with them. Sarai sat in the shade watching them all leave, disappear into the yards and houses where women had side pies waiting in the warming ovens.

The school drew Sarai with its promise and mystery, things the eager-to-be-gone children did not see. Sarai rode the pony toward the steps and dropped to the ground. She stretched up to look into the long glass windows.

"Can I help you?" asked a pleasant voice behind her. Sarai turned to find a young woman standing on the porch.

"I wanted to see inside," Sarai said. "I have never seen so fine a school. I cannot read much now, but I could once."

"Perhaps you will again. Come inside," said the teacher. "I will show you around."

Sarai stepped in and immediately to the side with her back against the rear wall. The teacher followed, generous and at ease in the familiar setting.

"In this room, I have eighteen students from ages six to fourteen. I keep the little ones up front near me so I can watch over them. Of course, the older students sit toward the back. They are very good to help with the little ones."

The teacher caught Sarai's arm and drew her down the aisle toward the front.

"The desks are new this year," she said, lifting a wooden desktop to disclose the spacious compartment for books and supplies. She frowned slightly. "Some of the children are better housekeepers than others," she said over the tumbled contents.

Sarai reached out for the reader, touching its cover with her finger tips.

"The desk is like the children's box, full of things to learn," she said.

198

"Yes, indeed," said the teacher. "Do you have children who will be coming here?"

"Not here," said Sarai. "Not yet. Too small, too far away. One day, maybe so."

"You're just shopping then," said the teacher.

"Shopping?" asked Sarai.

"Just looking around for possible future use."

"That is so," said Sarai. "Teacher, would you see something for me?"

Miss Garrett nodded.

Sarai went to the blackboard. She wrote carefully what she had written on the slate in her cabin: my name is Sarai Stone.

"The famous Sarai Stone?" asked the teacher. "My father, Judge Garrett, is very impressed with your riding and your generosity."

Sarai still looked at the blackboard.

"It is written well?" she asked.

Miss Garrett studied Sarai's concentration, then turned her attention to the writing.

"Well," she said, "I can read it very well. But you do need practice, some refinement. I might venture that it's the beginning of a fine hand . . . still child-like, but one day a fine hand. Come, I'll show you some exercises with pen and paper. You know penmanship is very important."

She and Sarai worked at the student desk, practicing ovals and push pulls. Sarai struggled with the pen, but concentrated on the paper.

"There, that's it," said Miss Garrett. "Excellent. You are a ready pupil."

Sarai smiled, looking at her ink-stained fingers and then at Miss Garrett's immaculate hands. She looked up.

"I have a letter. I can read some, but not much. Will you help me to read it?"

"Of course, Miss Stone," said the teacher.

Sarai hurried back to the pony and the saddle bags that held the letter. Miss Garrett followed. Sarai retrieved the letter and handed it to the teacher. Miss Garrett opened it carefully and removed the folded letter. She concentrated on the letter as Sarai looked about.

Suddenly Sarai straightened. "Whadi," she said, and ran toward her horse. The paint mare, Whadi, belonged to her youngest son, and Sarai saw it grazing peacefully in the stable yard down the street.

Holding the letter, Miss Garrett looked up as the woman whirled the horse and dashed toward the livery.

"It says the Old Place and all Silas Stone's other property and money are yours and . . . ," the teacher was saying, now to herself.

Sarai burst into the hotel lobby and went straight to the desk.

"A boy," she said. "Where is the Comanche boy?"

"Really, madam," the clerk said wearily, "does this look like the place you would find a Comanche Indian?"

"The stable man said the one who owns the horse came here," Sarai said.

"No *boy* has come in here. Not black. Not white. Not Comanche. No boy. Period. Some men came in a half hour ago and went into the bar back there. Wait!" he said as Sarai started for the back, "you can't go in there. Stop!"

He lifted the counter partition and started after her just as a party of guests came in. He lowered it again calmly as he greeted them.

Sarai opened the door with the etched glass panel.

The room had a long bar with a brass rail. Behind it hung a sparkling mirror that reflected the lights the barman was lighting. There were tables around the room with a few groups of men.

"Where is the one that rides the pinto with the scar on its neck?" Sarai asked from the door.

The men looked up, mildly curious at this intrusion and the question.

"Get out of here!" the barman barked. "Go on. Women ain't allowed back here. Git."

"The pinto. Who rides it?" Sarai persisted, ignoring the man who started toward her. He moved quickly and caught her by the arm.

"Let's go, sister," he said.

Sarai pressed the point of her knife against his fat, aproned belly.

"I will go when I find the rider," she said, very close to him.

"Let her be, Harry," a voice said from the corner table. "The horse is mine. I took it off a dead Comanch' myself. Genuine Indian pony if you want to buy."

Sarai's eyes ran over the man, separating him from the others. He was heavy and dark, a beard running around the lower half of his face into the matted black hair that sprouted from his filthy collar.

"You want proof?" the man said. "There." He threw a scalp on the green table top among the cards. "Fancy dude." He flicked the silver bells braided into the scalp lock with his forefinger.

"Aiy," Sarai shrieked and lunged past the barkeeper toward the scalp lock. She threw herself over the table at the bearded man, the knife flashing in her hand and Comanche words tumbling from her mouth.

The man's companions caught her and wrestled

her to the floor, ripping the knife from her hand, turning the table over and spilling the scalp, cards, and chips to the floor around her. Sarai fought, reached out for the hair.

"Damn," said one of the men as she bit his hand. He hit her hard as she tried to rise, sending her back against the floor. Sarai lay still, unconscious.

"What in the hell did you do to her, Del?"

"Damned if I know," said Del, picking up the scalp and setting up his chair. "It's getting so a man can't say nothin'. Sorry, for the trouble, boys. Harry, get her out of here."

Harry grabbed Sarai's wrists. He dragged her across the room through the lobby and toward the street door.

"Well, good heavens," the manager said, his voice rising out of control. "For heaven's sake why didn't you use the back door?"

"Shut up and give me a hand," Harry said, reaching for the door knob just as the door swung open.

Hugh Kane stood on the threshold looking down at the man bent over, pulling the unconscious woman. "Kane!" exclaimed the clerk.

Kane saw the woman was Sarai Stone as the bartender straightened up. He pushed him aside and picked up Sarai's limp body. He carried Sarai toward a settee against the back wall of the room. Laying her down, he looked up at the clerk.

"What the hell's been going on here? Spill it."

"I don't know. She came in here, looking for a Comanche boy. Said the stable man told her the owner of some Indian nag had come in here. I said there was no child. The only people who'd come in were in the bar. She broke in there brazen as brass and wouldn't leave when Harry asked her to."

"So he knocked her out?" asked Kane contemptuously.

"No," the shocked clerk said. "Certainly not. This is a reputable place. I didn't see what happened. I just heard a ruckus, and then Harry brought her out. She must have fainted."

"That's how she got that bruise on her face. Hell, man, I can see the knuckle prints."

"One of the patrons hit her," Harry said.

"Why?"

"She attacked him with a knife. Tried it on me first," Harry verified.

"Get the hell out of here," Kane said. "I'll talk to you later."

"Prelox," Sarai said and words in Comanche that made Kane frown. He drew up a chair and sat down, depositing his saddle bags and shotgun beside the settee. Kane gently stroked the tousled hair from her face. She hit him, and he held her.

"Settle down," Kane said. "Settle down. You've got a friend here. Easy."

He grabbed her hand as it swung out again. Her legs came off the settee kicking at him.

"No damn wonder they knocked you silly," he said, and threw his weight on top of her.

"Good heavens," the clerk said, looking about.

"Open your eyes, Sarai," Kane said. "Sarai!"

"Kane," she murmured as she looked at his face over her own. "He killed my child. Killed my son. Scalped him."

Kane felt sick. He released Sarai and stood up.

"Who did?" he asked.

"The man in the back. Del."

"Sarai," Kane said, trying to think, "you can't be sure of that."

"The horse. He rode in with Prelox's horse. He said he killed the Indian it belonged to and threw the scalp on the table to prove it," Sarai said.

"The boy could have traded the horse or loaned it to a man."

"No," Sarai said flatly. "I braided the bells into the scalp lock. One brass, two silver, one brass. And a cross."

Kane wiped his eyes with his fingertips. He knew she was right. The man had murdered the child. He had wanted the horse and killing an Indian child had meant nothing to him. Kane also knew the law wouldn't touch him. He sat down. Sarai's eyes searched his face.

Finding no answer, she turned away.

"I will kill him."

Kane took her shoulders and shook her.

"No, you won't. You're not a wild Comanche, any more. Nothing comes of killing but more killing. Give me a chance. Did he hit you?"

The thought of holding the killer for hitting a woman flickered across Kane's mind.

"No," she said listlessly. "When I bit the other man, he hit me. They took my knife, or I'd have killed him, too."

"How many did you tie into?" Kane smiled briefly at the thought.

"Just three." Sarai shook the hair out of her face. "He had the scalp. I am going to kill him."

"Sarai, I'll see what I can do. If I get the scalp back, will you be satisfied?"

Sarai did not look at him.

"He wears it in his belt," she said.

"Wait here."

Kane started across the lobby to the bar. The clerk trotted at his elbow.

"What's so big about a scalp?" he said.

"The Comanches believe that the scalp is sacred. The soul's in it. Without a scalp a warrior wanders forever between the winds. I've seen Comanches cut off their own braves' heads to keep an enemy from taking the scalp. If she can get it back, she can make an offering, get it back to the child, and he will live forever with his ancestors. One day she will see him again."

Kane opened the door. The room was filled. Harry stood behind the bar, talking intently to a couple of men. As Kane stepped through the door and stopped, the room became silent. Kane saw Harry lean forward and put his hand on the shotgun hidden under the bar.

That's one, Kane thought. He's warned and ready for me. Kane, you've acted stupid about this whole thing, played into their hands on their own ground because you got emotional.

The other men were mostly just casual drinkers, mildly curious about the unfolding events. Kane tried to see them all, judge the dangerous ones. His eyes came to rest on the threesome in the corner. They were genuine low-life. The bearded one had a smirk across his mouth. He knew he was safe. It galled Kane. He wanted to do exactly what Sarai wanted to do — kill the bastard.

"You have the scalp?" Kane asked.

"That's right. What you aim to do about it?" Del asked.

"I *aim* to ask you to give it up," said Kane, trying to keep the bartender in the corner of his eye.

"Why should I? I took it fair and square."

"You took it from a little boy who couldn't defend himself," Kane said.

"But you can, can't you?" said the man at the table.

"If I have to," Kane answered.

"You came in here to have to, didn't you?" said Del.

"Keep your hands above the table," Kane said.

"You heard him," Del said. "Making threats."

"Mister," Kane said, "I haven't made any threats. I've asked you nice for the child's scalp. It would mean a lot to the lady since it was her boy you killed. If you were a man, you'd give it back and the kid's horse, too."

"If you were a man, Squawman, you wouldn't ask for it for a Comanche's leavin's. She's been passed over the prairie by many a buck."

Kane stepped forward, fists tight at his sides.

"Give me the child's scalp, and I'll forget you said that."

"Squawman, I took this," Del shook the scalp, and Kane saw the bells and cross braided into it, "off a raging Comanche warrior. Real dude, that buck was." The man flicked the bells with his finger. "You just called me a liar by saying otherwise."

"Liar's what you are," Kane said quietly as the man shifted in his chair. "Keep your hands on the table, or you'll be a dead liar."

"He's goin' for his gun," the scalp man shouted loudly.

Kane had not reached. He saw the man roll onto the floor. At the same time, he felt a hot pain run down his neck, paralyzing his drawing arm.

Kane thought he saw the lights blown out by a sudden burst of wind from behind him. And then, he lay there on the floor of the San Jacinto saloon with the clerk standing over him holding a wooden mallet.

"Sheriff," the clerk said to the man who entered behind him, "that's him. The troublemaker. He threatened Mr. Cupid."

Chapter Twenty-Nine

From the settee in the dark corner of the lobby, Sarai saw the sheriff and two men carrying Kane's limp body from the bar. In the confusion and noise, she was forgotten. Quietly, Sarai lifted the double-barreled shotgun from Kane's gear dropped beside the couch. She moved against the flow of events up the stairs to the landing looking out on Front Street.

Below her, Sarai saw the two men carrying Kane across the street to the stone courthouse jail. They had him under the arms. His boot toes dug furrows in the dirt of the street. She watched, waited.

A movement below pulled her eyes away from Kane. The man who had taken her son's scalp walked down the street to the livery where she had seen the pinto. Sarai's hand tightened on the sill. There was noise in the hall, loud voices were coming up the stairs.

Sarai slipped through the open window onto the roof. In the shadows, she watched Del Cupid disappear into the stable and then reappear with the pinto. He rode away into the darkness. Sarai waited. The noise in the hall subsided. The lights of the town went out one by one. At last, Sarai jumped to a shed roof and climbed down from the roof of the San Jacinto Hotel. She found the gray and rode out after the man who killed and desecrated her son.

The campfire made a beacon across the flat plains as Del Cupid sighted down the barrel of his brand new pistol. "Bang," he said. "Bang, bang."

"Go to sleep, Del," the old man, wrapped in his bed roll, said. "We got an early start."

"Ain't sleepy, old man," said Cupid, as he set powder and lead balls into the chambers of the Colt and levered them down.

The old man grunted and rolled onto his side.

Cupid played with his new toy, examining the brass powder flash and caps in the wooden box.

"By god, this is a nice rig . . . mighty nice, a beautiful damn killing machine."

When Cupid looked up, Sarai Stone sat on the gray at the edge of the circle of light. Kane's shotgun lay across the withers, barrel toward him.

"Holly hell," the child killer said under his breath. "Where in hell did she come from? How? Like a damned Injun, sure enough."

Sarai did not get down, said nothing, but sat looking at the man who inched back from the fire, holding the pistol in the shadow against his thigh. Cupid could not tell what she was thinking. Her face was passive and calm. She made no move with the shotgun.

The old man raised himself on his elbow.

"What's goin' on?" he asked.

"Shut up!" Cupid said. A smile began to grow on his swarthy face. "She ain't so bad looking," he said to the old man. "Bet she knows plenty about pleasing a man, living with the Indians like she done." To Sarai, he said, "You want this?" He waved the scalp, teasing her.

"Yes," she said softly.

"What'll you give me? A little of what you gave them Comanch' bucks. Just a little of that." Cupid licked his lips, rubbed his left hand between his legs. "We may

208

have us a party, old man. Big party on the ground. How about it, honey?"

Sarai set without moving.

"Well, maybe you want me to come over and take it."

Sarai did not move.

A thought flickered across Del Cupid's mind. Cupid was a buffalo hunter and wolfer because he enjoyed killing. He liked to see the big buffalo five hundred yards away drop to their knees and roll to the ground in quick succession, never knowing where the shots came from. He liked seeing the wolves crawl on their poisoned bellies tormented by the pain of their dying.

"Well, you call the tune, honey. I'd just as soon kill you. Both ways is good for me. Want to know how I got this?" Cupid's smile was bigger. "This kid came into my camp just like you. Rode right in, rubbing his stomach like he wants eats. I looked at that pinto. I always wanted a pinto. I raised my gun like this. . . ."

Cupid's thumb pulled back the hammer slowly as he raised the shining new gun from his side.

Before he fired, even as his finger closed over the trigger, Sarai shot him in the chest without raising the shotgun. Cupid slammed back against his saddle, a gaping hole blown through his heart.

At the percussion the gray pitched up on her back and then came quickly down. Sarai swung the gun over at the other man. He jerked his hands up high over his head.

She lowered the gun, but kept her finger on the trigger. Slowly Sarai rode forward through the camp. Without dismounting, bending from the waist, she took the scalp lock from Del Cupid's dead fingers.

At the camp edge, she pulled the tie rope on the pinto. Then Sarai kicked the mare, and they disappeared into the blackness.

By the time Kane's head cleared and Judge Garrett had him out of jail, it was nearly daylight. Kane ignored the clerk as he picked up his gear from the floor of the hotel lobby.

"She isn't here," the clerk said knowingly. "She stole your shotgun and disappeared last night. Must have gotten away in all the confusion. Here's a bill for the damages you caused to the saloon."

Kane came over to the counter, putting on his dusty hat and throwing the saddle bags over his shoulder.

"Sue me," he said and walked out.

Kane cut across country toward the Yancey place. He figured Sarai wouldn't leave Summer for long. The familiar creaks of leather and the horse's steady breathing in the easy canter sung softly to his senses. Miles passed unnoticed until he rode down a wash and up into a hackberry grove. Under the trees, Kane espied an old man, sitting by a fire, drinking coffee. He was looking across thoughtfully at Del Cupid's body sprawled against a log.

"Mess, ain't it?" the old man said flatly, without turning to look at Kane. "I always got to clean up after Del. Reckon this'll be the last time, though."

"Who did it?" Kane asked, knowing the answer.

The old man talked at his own pace.

"When I woke up, there was this woman on a horse sitting where you are, about. He waved his scalp in her face and was showing her how he got it with that new pistol. Before he pulled the trigger, she kilt him.

Aiy God, she was stony. Took the scalp and the horse, and left. That was it. Oh, I left out the lewd remarks Del was makin'. Care for some coffee?"

Kane did not hear the question. He spurred off toward Sarai's farm. As he rode in, he saw his shotgun leaning against the bright yellow gypsy wagon. Della stood up. She'd been waiting for him.

"She's gone," the black woman said, tears running from her eyes. "Took the baby and gone. 'Can't be no white person,' she said. Get down, Mr. Kane, eat you some breakfast. Rest your horse. She's long gone."

"You know where she went?" Kane asked, dismounting the lathered horse.

"Out to the Injuns," Della said. "I thought she was goin' to make it yesterday when she went off to get her name writing. She'd been talkin' about her boys . . . how they had to learn to read and write to stand up to the white folks. I didn't know she had two boys beside the little girl till yesterday."

Della shook her head.

Kane wasn't listening closely to what she was saying. He was trying to think, sort things out. "Did you see the scalp?"

Della shook her head. "No, sir. Scalp? No." Della thought about Kane's question. "She wrapped something real careful in buckskin from her saddle bags. Put it away tender by the little book. She give Jack the deed, the cash money, and say pay the taxes, and they can't run you off. Say you have any troubles you ask the school teacher, Miss Garrett, or Judge Garrett hisself. She didn't take much just some food for the baby, a canteen of water and the dried tobacco leaves Jack had hanging on the wagon."

Jack came out the door and stood on the porch, listening.

"Which way did she go?"

"Out that away . . . ," Jack answered, "north and a little west."

Della wiped her face with her white apron.

Kane looked where Jack pointed. "The Comanches won't be there this time of year." His mind raced through what he knew, what Della and Jack had said. "She's going to the mounds to bury her son, free his soul."

"Bury her son?" Della said softly.

"What mounds?" said Jack.

"Medicine Mounds," Kane said absently. "Four hills way out on the prairie. Comanches think they're sacred. By God, that's where she's headed. That's why she took the tobacco . . . for an offering, sweet smoke."

Kane started back toward his horse.

"Mr. Kane, let her be," Della said, coming up quickly and touching his arm. "She ain't happy here. I love her like my life and want to keep her. But she ain't happy here, ain't free like she wants to be."

Kane squeezed Della's hand.

"I've got to find her, Della. One last time, I have to take her back."

Della dropped her head forward.

"She don't want back."

"Back to her husband," Kane clarified.

Della looked up.

Kane smiled.

"This may work out, after all," he said.

Kane left Della and Jack after that, heading north and a little west at an easy pace. He knew where he was going, and the horse needed the rest. He rode for three days. Riding across the empty land beyond the farms and towns gave him time to think. He hadn't thought very clearly in the last week. There was time now. At Jacksboro, he stopped for supplies. He found no sign of Sarai, but he knew where she was going.

On the fourth day, Kane spotted the dust behind him. He watched closely through his field glasses as five men rode along his trail. Kane thought as he remounted the horse. News must have reached Jacksboro behind him of Sarai's killing of Del Cupid. The men were watching his trail. He hadn't bothered to hide it. They were lawmen, or they were Del Cupid's cussed buffalo-hunter cronies, looking for revenge. Either way Kane knew he and the woman were in trouble if he led them to her.

Kane cut off back down his trail and then along a stream bed, and across and back again across a rocky flat until he was sure he had confused the pursuers. Then he kicked the horse into an easy canter and set off after Sarai again.

On the fifth day, Kane saw the mounds rising blue out of the flat land a long way off, a day's ride nearly looking at the sacred hills. Once he thought he saw a tiny rider ahead. Nothing he could see rode behind him now. He continued at the easy, steady pace.

It was twilight as he picked his way around the bases of the mounds, looking for Sarai. A coyote called far off in the silence. Another answered, and another. And then, in the eternal stillness without man, Kane heard the eerie, heart-freezing cry of the Comanche death song.

Following the keening in the night air, he found the horses hobbled near a small fire between the hills. Summer lay asleep, covered by a bright saddle blanket, pillowed on Sarai's shawl. Her hair was cropped off below the ears. A pile of cut hair, hers and Sarai's, lay on the ground. Kane dismounted, looking up the side of the highest hill. The song of grief washed down the sides over him. Kane looped his gunbelt over the saddle horn and put his hat on top. It was a sacred place.

Slowly he climbed the platform to the sky. The wailing sounds of sorrow grew louder, though they were soft sounds. Kane smelled the smoke of the offering fire acrid in the fresh night air. When he reached the top, he saw Sarai.

She sat with her back toward him. Her arms were stretched up high over her head, holding the tobacco leaves and the glistening knife. The beaded saddle bag lay open with the book and an empty piece of buckskin spilled on the ground.

Kane watched silently, intently. Sarai's arm, holding the knife, came down in front of her, and then the one holding the tobacco. She threw the knife against the saddle bag, wiped the leaves against her body and mourned, softly bending over her knees. She pulled herself up and one by one she lay the broad leaves on the fire and watched the smoke rise toward the heavens.

"Do not stay between the winds, my son. Rest with The People in green valleys. Ride your pony joyfully again. Elimah, receive my son for me."

Kane moved quietly to see better what Sarai was doing. A rock skipped over the ground. Sarai moved at the same time, putting the fire between her and Kane. In the flickering light that danced over her body, Kane saw the blood flowing from deep gashes on her chest and arms. He closed his eyes.

In the trance-like grief of the death song, Sarai had slashed her own body repeatedly, and wiped away the blood with the tobacco leaves. Then she offered the leaves, a sweet smelling sacrifice, for her son's spirit. She wove slightly before the fire, weak from her fast, the journey, the blood loss, and her grief.

"It is done, Kane," she said as he came forward and kneeled beside the spilled saddle bag. Kane looked at the bloody knife, red with the woman's blood. "I will not go back."

"I don't want you to," Kane said quietly, looking up. "I'm taking you home . . . back to Nobah and the Comanches."

Sarai wiped the tears from her eyes.

"He is alive?" she said softly.

"He is alive," Kane said.

"My other son?" she asked.

"I don't know that," Kane said. "But I've been commissioned to bring you and Summer back. Then I must go and find him."

"Commissioned?"

"Nobah sent me to get you. The deal is, you and the children for my friend, Logan. This is sure a strange turn around."

Sarai stood up. She quickly gathered the bag near Kane's feet and started down the hill to the baby and the horses. Kane followed.

"We don't have to go this minute," he said.

"Yes, we do," Sarai said. "There are five riders only a day and a half behind you. Did you not see them?"

"I saw them," Kane said. "I lost them."

"You did not lose them," Sarai said, looking at Kane

across the back of her horse. "You are not good at such things. But I will lose them, *gringo*."

A smile darted across her face at the last word.

"I must go home."

IN MEDIAS RES